HELEN GLOWACKI

ANGELS

ALIENS &

CHARIOTS

WILL NEW DISCOVERIES BREAK OUR FAITH?

by

Helen Glowacki

Novels by Helen Glowacki

When God Broke Grandma's Heart
When God Took Grandma Home
When Grandma Chased the Spirits
The Granddaughter and the Monkey Swing
The Story of God's Plan of Salvation
Abiding Faith, Hidden Treasure
And Then They Asked God
Caleb's Testimony

Why God Why Series by Helen Glowacki

To What Purpose?
Why God Why?
Why Trust Scripture?
Life after Death And The Coming Tribulation
What Does God Want Me To Do RIGHT NOW?
Do Our Little Sins *Really* Count?
What Do Angels Do?
What is Faith?
Satan's Gift of Fear

Other non-fiction Books by Helen Glowacki

Politically Incorrect: The Get Some Gumption
Handbook When Enough is Enough
Overcoming Depression: How to be Happy
What No One Is Telling You about Addictions
Angels, Aliens and Chariots

Authors Website: www.helenglowacki.com

ANGELS

ALIENS &

CHARIOTS

WILL NEW DISCOVERIES BREAK OUR FAITH?

by

Helen Glowacki

HELEN GLOWACKI

Copyright © August 2017 by Helen Glowacki
Library of Congress Control Number:
ISBN   Softcover: ISBN 978-0-9893-8079-9
        EBook: ISBN978-0-9913-9162-2

Non-fiction books by Helen Glowacki are facts as gleaned from scripture and other sources and presented according to her research, opinion, religious beliefs and personal interpretation. Novels by Helen Glowacki are works of fiction and references to real people, events, organizations, or locales are intended only to provide a sense of authenticity and are used fictionally. All other characters and all incidents and dialogue are drawn from the author's imagination and are not to be construed as real. Any resemblance to actual persons, living or dead is entirely coincidental.

This book was printed in the United States of America

The King James Version (KJV) of the Bible, which is public domain in the United States of America, has been used for all scriptural references throughout this book. The application of which is based upon the opinion, research and religious belief of the author.

Cover assembly by DR Designs, West Palm Beach, Florida
Scriptural Index assembled by Jayden Ruiter, Enbrum, Ontario, Canada

To order additional copies of this book visit
www.helenglowacki.com or Amazon.com

<u>MISSION STATEMENT</u>

To Serve

God

With

All Our Strength

And

All Our Heart

Helen Glowacki

DEDICATION

This book is dedicated to

TOM & TERRY CECIL

Palm Coast, Florida

WILLIAM DANNENBERGER

St. Louis, Missouri

ED AND JACKIE RUITER

Ontario, Canada

For their assistance in the critique,

accuracy, and/or editing

of this material

NOTE TO THE READER

The non-fiction books by Helen Glowacki represent the opinion, research, religious beliefs and scriptural interpretations of the author and not meant to be used in lieu of the advice of ministerial, theological, medical or psychological experts. No part of these books may be used or reproduced in any manner whatsoever without written permission except in the case of brief quotations embodied in critical articles and reviews.

The novels by Helen Glowacki are works of fiction. While some events in these novels reflect the expertise of those in particular vocations, or reflect the sequence of events found in some legal matters, or the workings of various home owner associations, references to real people, events, organizations, or locales are intended only to provide a sense of authenticity, and are used fictitiously. Characters, incidents and dialogue are drawn from the author's imagination and are not to be construed as real. Any resemblance to actual persons, living or dead is entirely coincidental.

The King James Version (KJV) of the Bible, which is public domain in the United States, is used throughout the books by this author. For further study, the author recommends the New King James Version (NKJV) of the Bible as easier reading and less usage of the old world language while remaining true to the original text.

"One thing have I desired

of the Lord,

that I will seek after;

that I may dwell

in the house of the Lord

all the days of my life,

to behold the beauty of the Lord,

and to enquire in his temple."

Psalm 27: 4

ACKNOWLEDGEMENTS

Special thanks to all those who encouraged me to develop Scriptural Insight, Inc., a new charitable foundation through which we can now send my books and articles all over the world. Thanks to our board members: Jerry Saperstein, Danny Landolfi, Ed Ruiter, Beth Jansen, and Janek Puljanowski for their love, advice and encouragement and to Irina Najinsky for all her computer wisdom. Special thanks to Wally who vigorously supported my work, made my computer behave, and gave me the precious gift of unconditional love and now to Janek as well, who came into my life just when I needed him!

Thanks to my children and grandchildren and to Janeks children and grandchildren for the constancy of their love and support. Thanks to the late Reverend Herold Ambroise for his fervent prayers for which I am so grateful. Thanks to Richard Levinson for giving me the opportunities to develop my writing skills and to believe in myself. Thanks to Jy Oh for her assistance with the materials we send to other countries. Thanks to my Face Book friends who provide me with their prayers and supportive posts! But most of all, my heartfelt, humble thanks to our Heavenly Father for His inspiration, guiding hand, protection, and never-ending love. May this work bring joy to His heart and help find that last soul!

"And the Spirit, and the bride say,

Come.

And let him that heareth say,

Come,

and let him that is athirst,

Come.

And whosoever will,

let him take the water of life

freely."

Revelation 22:17

INTRODUCTION

I've long been curious about why scripture contains so many references to fear. I've felt that there must be more to this emotion; more to what can cause this emotion than meets the eye when it comes to our faith. Thus, I wondered if I could learn why God mentions fear so often throughout scripture.

From a strict Biblical viewpoint, the word fear refers to giving God the reverence and worship commensurate to His perfection and power. There are approximately 118 verses in scripture where this type of fear is mentioned. However, there is another type of fear God describes which is mentioned 365 times in scripture and which this book will address.

To give the reader a feel for how these two different meanings of the word fear is applied throughout scripture I will first list a few of those verses which address God's admonition to fear/worship Him.

Genesis 22:12 tells us: *".....Now I know that you fear God....".* Exodus 1:21 explains: *"....because the midwives feared God..."* Exodus 14:21 admits: *"....the people feared the Lord."* Exodus 20:20 tells us: *"...so that the fear of God will be with you..."* Leviticus 19:14 admonishes: *"...but fear your God."* Jeremiah 5:22 asks: *"....should you not fear me....tremble in my presence?"* Proverbs 1:7 explains: *"The fear of the Lord is the beginning of knowledge".* And Psalms111:10 *backs up the last verse with the words: "The fear of the Lord is the beginning of wisdom."*

These 118 verses found throughout scripture in Genesis, Exodus, Leviticus, Deuteronomy, Joshua, 1 Samuel, 2 Samuel, 1 Chronicles, 2 Chronicles, Nehemiah, Job, Psalms, Proverbs, Ecclesiastes, Isaiah, Jeremiah, Daniel, Jonah, Zephaniah, Malachi, Luke, Acts, 2 Corinthians, Ephesians, Philippians, Hebrews, 1 Peter and Revelation certainly prove their importance by the breathe and scope of their inclusion in the Bible. They are to teach us to develop an awe of our Heavenly Father. Without this we cannot know or please Him.

Without a Biblical fear of God we have either disregarded, or are ignorant of, the rule of righteousness in God's Plan of Salvation. God will always guide the ignorant to His word but those who know and disregard it will be responsible for possibly losing their soul salvation. However, in the context of this book, I refer only to the many times God speaks of the fear which we face in our daily lives and how God tells us not to worry about what we encounter in life because He *sees* all and *controls* all.

Thus, as I mentioned earlier, I became curious about what those fears and circumstances are which could be so daunting that we could easily lose our faith over them. Were these events in the past or in the future? Is the fear produced from within ourselves or brought on by external circumstances and if so…what?

Exploring scripture to find some of the answers to my questions, and examining the events of our time, and events past, I have come to recognize that we do have, and have had, much to fear. God is telling us it is only through our faith in Him that will we overcome fear. Scripture also tells us that it will be our **lack of knowledge** concerning the Bible, our lack of understanding God's Plan of Salvation, possibly even our misapplication of previous information which could be our downfall.

In thinking about how I personally feel about this revelation and wondering what I might yet need to do to face a future traumatic event, I realized that most of us have constructed a belief system by which we work, and play, and worship. When we examine that system we can see that we have probably built a very confining concept of what we will believe and what we will not believe. We have become set in a specific way of worship; comfortable with what we have accepted as true and what we have kept locked away. We do not like change because we are content as we are and change would cause an upheaval to the arena of comfort we have worked so hard to develop. Therefore we find it troubling to think too deeply about allowing our established faith or lack of faith to change direction.

Since we simply brush aside that which makes us uncomfortable and does not fit into the fenced areas we have constructed, we have instead embraced that which fits our concepts and discarded that which does not. We carefully guard our constructed ideas and do not want to consider changing them.

However, scripture defines this way of thinking as being "hard hearted", or to have a "hardened heart". These words are used very often throughout scripture when describing mankind's refusal to learn God's words, admit that we may be wrong, may have misunderstood God's words, or even denigrated God's role in our lives. When this occurs we do not open our hearts and our minds enough to fully understand what God wants to tell us and thereby we deny our fullest potential for learning. Being hard-hearted, in its Biblical meaning tells us that we have **an inability to comprehend spiritual truth.**

Ephesians 4:18 warns: *"They are darkened in their understanding, alienated from the life of God because of the ignorance that is in them, due to their **hardness of heart**."*

Matthew 13:15 teaches: *"For this people's heart has grown dull, and with their ears they can barely hear, and their eyes they have closed, lest they should see with their eyes and hear with their ears and **understand with their heart** and turn, and I would heal them.'*

And Romans 2:5 explains: *"But because of your **hard and impenitent heart** you are storing up wrath for yourself on the day of wrath when God's righteous judgment will be revealed."*

Most of us already acknowledge that we are living in the end times, in an era where we are witnessing the conclusion of God's Plan of Salvation for mankind, yet we still resist opening our hearts to the importance of God's warnings. Even when we recognize that Christianity will move into its final phase of God's Plan of Salvation and evil will increase in power and vehemence, we do not seek to increase our knowledge of God's plan for our lives.

We may accept the warnings scripture brings us about the "end times" when God's children will come under a satanic attack which can break what little faith we have. We may understand that Satan's goal is to prolong his life and escape being thrown into the Lake of Fire by *preventing* God from completing His plan of salvation. And still we do not give God's words the importance they deserve.

Yet God, in His long suffering, and His immense love and understanding, patiently warns us through scripture that *conquering our fear will be an important component to remaining faithful.* Further, God warns quite strongly that **many Christians will be lost from *a lack of knowledge.***

Therefore, we must learn what it is that we still lack or what exactly can break our faith.

Most of us know that Satan can influence the thoughts and belief systems of ordinary, even god-fearing people, and **has the power to blind the hearts and minds of men** and confuse their thought process. Despite this, we somehow don't envision our faith being seriously damaged by this. Nor do we consider that *our faith could be challenged so fiercely that we could even lose our soul salvation.*

Nevertheless, scripture clearly tells us that God places a great deal of importance on our fear. It is this point which causes me to wonder what could cause such a fear. Thus I wanted to examine some *past* events which may have challenged our faith and possibly brought a great fear to our heart.

Approximately 50-60 years ago when it became common knowledge that concentration camps wrought by World War 11 had killed millions of people and inflicted terrible horrors on men women and children, some felt their faith challenged. Many wondered why God did not intervene especially when scripture describes the Jews as God's favored people! Many felt that God didn't care about the atrocities which prevailed and questioned why He did not appear to respond to the dire needs of the very people He created.

When Darwin brought forth his Theory of Evolution many felt their faith challenged. When discoveries were made about how advanced the science and technology of ancient civilizations appeared to be, many felt their faith challenged.

When hieroglyphics depicted the "gods" worshipped by ancient civilizations as apparently visiting them from outer space, many felt their faith challenged. Further, many Christians were stunned as huge pyramids were found all across the entire world making this a **universal** occurrence. Others wondered how the people of these ancient civilizations knew how to build such huge edifices and how to align their buildings to the stars.

These few incidents alone initially shook the very tenets of Christianity. But throughout scripture God's concern about our fear and our lack of knowledge does not seem to be referring only to past events, but to events occurring *or which **will occur*** during the end times in which we now live. If so, we need to peruse scripture more carefully with an eye toward why we might battle a debilitating fear in the future and why we suffer from what God calls a "lack of knowledge". What do we need to learn?

Our responses to the few events just mentioned force us to acknowledge that there is so much we do not know and so many questions still unanswered. From this we can conclude that a "lack of knowledge" clearly does exist. But if God want us to better understand scripture, why...and what is it that we need to learn? What have we missed which worries our Heavenly Father?

We can also ask what did God feel when entire civilizations worshipped other gods? Could it be possible that these civilizations did obtain their technologies from the "gods" who visited them from the heavens? Was our Heavenly Father somehow helpless when Hitler perpetrated his atrocities...especially on those mentioned in scripture as God's favored people, the Jews?

Why did God wait so long to send Christ to mankind? What purpose might these past events have served in God's plan? What should we learn from the past which we could apply to our present circumstances? Is there something we are supposed to learn from God's handling of these past events? Were past events a part of the lessons we need to learn for facing future events? Were they precursors to what we may experience in the future and a warning about how new events might impact our faith?

As we review even the few events mentioned, we are forced to question the timing of God's revelation, of Christ's coming, and of what all this information should mean to us. These thoughts bring deeper questions about doubt and about the fear which doubt could spawn. They bring the realization that with so much new information about our world being unveiled; about what we are learning about past civilizations, about newly released information which was originally classified to prevent panic in the general population; we realize that *there is so much that we do not know.*

But are those events important? I believe that their importance lies in how we can or cannot "fit" them into our concept of what our faith dictates. Perhaps God is leading us to a greater understanding of the past to allow us to quell the fears we may develop in the future as even more spectacular events unfold. Perhaps we may soon face a crisis for which God wants us prepared.

To circumvent the doubt and fear of considering past events is why I decided to write this book and demonstrate through scripture how yesterdays' phenomenon can be explained and used for today. It is because of God's loving nature, His all knowing and all seeing capabilities that He has provided us with the answers to questions which arise about times past, about the times in which we now live, and about the times which we still face. God works through scripture and through the inspiration of the Holy Spirit. Thus, through scripture I believe God will provide what we need so we will *not be afraid* and will have what we need to maintain our faith as His Plan of Salvation is fulfilled. God wants us to overcome our fears, learn of His plan and trust Him *no matter how our previous and current concepts must change.*

God tells us that while scripture may remain be a mystery to many, His words will be understood by and an awakening for those who seek to grow their faith and become a part of God's new kingdom. God desires that *all* men be saved and clearly tells us that those who will be lost will do so because of their lack of knowledge **and the hardness of their heart which closes them off from the understanding they require.** God tells us emphatically in Malachi 3:10: *"Bring ye all the* *tithes into the storehouse, that there may be meat in mine house, and **prove me now herewith, saith the LORD of hosts, if I will not open you the windows of heaven**, and pour you out a blessing, that there shall not be room enough to receive it.*" What this verse tells us is that God invites us to challenge Him for answers and if we have a faithful heart He will "open the windows of Heaven" for us. However, the condition for His responding to our request is that we must "bring the tithes", meaning we must first demonstrate our faithfulness and obedience to His word. He does not open the windows of scripture for those who are unworthy to learn because they seek to find fault, will mock the information or even willfully disregard it.

But when we come to God with a pure heart, I believe that He will provide the answers we need and help us weather the coming storm. I believe that as new information and new technologies unfold, as the world slips into a place of terror, *we will be called upon not only to learn, but to teach and comfort others.* We must be patient and trust that no matter how dire a situation or how a new slant on life may seem to be, God is with us, we will be protected and God will create a blessing from these circumstances. God's decisions and actions, past and present, are and have always been perfect and ***purposeful!*** Therefore we must understand that patience, trust and obedience are important to our growth process. However, **God must act within the limits of the law of righteousness** under which He has **chosen** to labour so Satan will not have the opportunity to accuse Him of affecting man's free will to choose between good and evil.

I believe that God is warning us NOW that fear and anxiety may break our faith and that only a strong working knowledge of His words can save us. We are entering a new information era to which we must adapt. This information may shake our faith in God and make us doubt the hope and salvation offered through Christ. But, armed with what scripture forewarns, we will be strengthened as we realize God is so much more than we ever thought possible. There **IS** an explanation for everything and there **ARE** explanations throughout scripture which we must find to prevent us having the "lack of knowledge" God fears can cause us to lose our faith. We must understand how fear works in our bodies, and strive to learn God's plan to help us control our fears and doubts. We must trust God's admonition to find salvation *through our knowledge,* of God's words....and through prayer.

And finally we must understand that God *can and will* say to many, *"I know ye not"*! Those are words which none of us ever want to hear. We must remember that the five foolish and the five wise believers gathered together, eagerly awaited the Lord, thought they were prepared, and desired to go with Him when He came. But when the five foolish virgins were found to have their lamps only half filled with the amount of oil required, they had to leave to replenish their lamps. When they returned with the oil they were required to have, they were shocked to learn that the door had been closed and they could not go with the Lord. When they called to Him asking that the door be opened, they heard only the words: *"I know ye not"!* (Matthew 25:1-13) How devastating that must have been!

I hope each proponent of this book will arm us with what we need to learn so we can remain faithful during the final phase of God's plan for mankind. What you are about to read addresses the extent of God's power **and our difficulty understanding how far reaching that power is**. Now, as we reach the culmination of God's Plan of Salvation, we must demonstrate that we can accept *__new__* wisdom about God's plan, and adapt to how God works to bring mankind and all His creatures to the highest peak of growth possible. We must strive to discern the spirits by carefully watching for what is from God and what is not. It may be *__time for us to allow God to be more than we have allowed Him to be in the past.__* I hope we will obtain the wisdom and knowledge God longs to give us. I hope you enjoy this book and that the information will be new, helpful, and uplifting in its scope. God is opening more of the mysteries of scripture just when we are ready to understand, ready to stand firm and trust Him as His plan of Salvation comes to fruition! May God bless you and keep you always and may He touch your heart with the desire to learn of Him.

Helen Glowacki

TABLE OF CONTENTS

Chapter 12:

The Lord hath appeared

of old unto me,

saying Yea,

I have loved thee with

an everlasting love:

therefore with lovingkindness

have I drawn thee.

Jeremiah 31:3

Chapter One

THE POWER AND PSYCHE OF FEAR

In addition to the 185 verses about the need to fear God, which in essence means to worship Him, there are 365 verses in scripture telling us not to fear the circumstances we face in life. The 185 verses provide us with a warning while the 365 verses which we will address in this chapter offer words of comfort and reassurance. Thus God is concerned about how the emotion of fear affects us and wants to teach us how to overcome this response by having faith in His protection.

What is fear?

Fear, arising from the sudden awareness that there is a threat to our well being, is the most debilitating emotion we can feel. Whether related to our physical body or our emotional state, fear will trigger a sudden desire to either run from what threatens us, or face it and fight. When a threat is detected, the body releases adrenalin which provides the body with the strength to take immediate protective action.

A hormone called nor-epinephrine is also released to augment our preparation for flight or fight by shifting blood from the central part of the body to the extremities. The body then goes through a series of events after which another hormone, one called cortisol is released to maintain fluid balance and blood pressure. This totality of hormonal activity can be detrimental to the body if the situation continues because it can cause an inflammation which can be the underlying cause of heart disease, arthritis, cancer and other serious health problems. A lack of knowledge about the state of fear can prevent us from overcoming its debilitating effects.

What controls fear?

Initially, we cannot control the fear response because the brain is equipped with the automatic ability to store memories of both pleasant and unpleasant experiences. The lower part of the brain stem retains these memories to protect us from a threat to our well being or lead us toward what we enjoy. This area of the brain is called the Amygdala. To change this automatic response requires a working knowledge of and a new memory instilled into the brain of what will happen if we do not respond to a particular sensation of fear. This area of the brain also causes our heart to beat and our lungs to breathe without a conscious order from us to do so.

Similarly, our reaction to a threat is instantaneous and does not require us to first assess what we see, hear or feel, or issue an order to the body to react. The information or memory sent from the Amygdala to the rest of the body is instantaneous and does not require any thought from us. Even pleasure will cause us to react without thought unless we consciously command our thoughts in a different direction.

Why do we feel fear?

The Amygdala's automatic memory mechanism exists as a protective measure for mankind. It protects man from a harmful situation because it is spontaneous and does not require a thought process before acting. However, the Amygdala can create a memory, an automatic response, from erroneous information. This can produce *continued fear reactions which are not conducive to our well being and can evolve into anxiety and anxiety attacks.* While fear is a natural part of the Adam-like nature which relies only on self and reacts instantaneously, (without thought) to protect man from physical harm, this response can be reversed when the Amygdala is re-trained to respond to certain stimuli in a different manner.

How can we overcome fear?

Conversely, the self-less Christ-like nature, encourages a confidence born of faith and can help us combat fear. Trust in God's protection over us and in His plan for us promotes what I term *reasoning with assurance* by utilizing the neo-cortex section of the brain where reason and logic take precedence and helps re-train the Amygdala. Believing that God is fully aware of our dilemma and trusting that He will help us, produces a quelling effect which subdues fear. Believing that God understands our struggle to trust in His protection while we wrestle our fear strengthens us. Reading God's words of comfort throughout scripture teaches us that God does not want us to be fearful.

What is the main component of fear?

Whether for a short time or a longer period of time, fear can overwhelm us when the brain signals a threat to our well being. Fear triggers a great and sometimes overwhelming anxiety which can cause heart palpitations, profuse sweating, weakness, and many other unpleasant physical responses. Interestingly, studies reveal that a lack of knowledge about the source and power behind our fear can exacerbate the sensation of fear and lead to the inability to function properly. Conversely, knowledge about what is attacking us and why, can greatly reduce the disabling effects of fear. Hosea 4:6 in the Holy Bible warns that many will lose their soul salvation through a lack of knowledge. *"My people are destroyed for lack of knowledge, because thou hast rejected knowledge, **I will also reject thee** that thou shalt be no priest to me, seeing that thou hast forgotten the law of thy God, I will also forget my children,"*

Many areas of the Bible offer words which explain that under God's protection there is no reason to fear anything. In Proverbs 29:25 Gods tells us:

"The fear of man bringeth a snare, but whoso putteth his trust in the Lord shall be safe."

Did Biblical figures experience and overcome fear?

There are many stories in scripture about those who were placed into dire circumstances in Biblical times and were able to overcome their fears by trusting God. Daniel quite calmly stayed overnight in a den of lions. The young David who was later to become King went into combat against the well-known giant and famed soldier, Goliath. Shadrach, Meshach and Abednego were thrown into a fiery furnace and came out unscathed. Joshua and his small band of soldiers conquered entire cities.

As the Adam-like nature moves toward a trust in God, a change takes place in how we look at life and the events which occur around us. The fears stored in the Amygdala can be replaced by the trust we place in God through a new faith- based in knowledge which is derived by remembering our experiences of faith. However, fear is healthy and not to be misjudged. It is a protective measure important to the safety of man, but God explains that *__we must not be subject to our fears,__* not allow them free rein. We must be aware that Satan can use our fears to break our faith.

Sometimes we can quell the fear or the reactions which occur from a perceived threat as soon as we recognize that we needn't be afraid, and that what we perceived was a threat was actually harmless. Other times we can place our fear in God's hands through the power of prayer and trust in the outcome through the faith of trusting God. God's words of comfort and explanation are paramount to our ability to overcome our reactions of fear.

Further supporting the importance of obtaining knowledge is the parable of the five wise and the five foolish virgins. All ten were faithful, all desired to be with God, all had obtained "knowledge" which was evidenced by the fact that they all had oil in their lamps and had gathered at their designated meeting place. But the five foolish virgins had not acted on God's words thus did not follow through on God's admonitions to continually keep their lamps filled with the oil of God's words. The knowledge God offered them would have prepared them to be ready when God called.

Sadly, they would not listen, were lackadaisical and lacked the "oil" required for them to move forward. Thus they were left behind and only the five wise virgins were admitted into God's kingdom.

John 8:44-45 warns against not acting on the importance of what God tells us: *"Ye are of your father the devil....and because I tell you the truth,* ***ye believe me not.****"*On the other hand God loves us so much that he offers us the comfort of the words found in Joshua 1:9 where God says: *"Have I not commanded you? Be strong and of good courage; be not dismayed: For the Lord God is with thee wherever thou goest."*

1 Corinthians 2:9 explains, *"Eye hath not seen, not ear heard, neither have entered into the heart of man, the things which God hath prepared for them that love Him"*. This clearly tell us that we have a

long way to go to obtain a complete understanding of God's immense plan of Salvation and what that plan brings to our future. In Luke 22:32 God says: *"But I have prayed for thee, that thy faith fail not....."*

God does not want us to fear. Fear and its debilitating components come from Satan while hope, trust and faith come from God. It is important that we acknowledge this and associate fear with the work of Satan. Satan has the power to *"move men to do his bidding"* (1 Chronicles 21:1), *can cause illness* (Job 2:7), *can take God's word from men's heart's* (Mark 4:15), *can blind the minds of them which believe not* (2 Corinthians4:4), *can send messengers to hurt man* (2 Corinthians 12:7), *can produce signs and wonders* (2 Thessalonians 2:9) and has a host of other powers as well.

While most of us have seen the face of evil; been a victim of evil doers. and may have lived through a blatantly evil event or even one so subtle that we were stunned when it was upon us, we still cannot fathom the depths evil will go to thwart God's plan for mankind. As documented by history, evil has existed even longer than mankind has lived. Scripture warns that during the end times evil will increase in power as Christianity moves into its final phase of God's Plan of Salvation. Evil can produce fear while scripture can help us deal with what we see, hear or experience which is intended to add to our fear. Scripture teaches us how to protect ourselves from what Satan will do.

When a child burns their hand on a hot stove, they remember not to touch the stove again. Thus it is our "experiences" which help us avoid future harm. But it is also our "experiences" which help us recognize the power and majesty of God and give us those memories of God's help to develop our faith, to trust Him and therefore overcome our fear.

Fear which has been born of a bad experience which we have seen, felt, or heard and or born of the unknown is "remembered" by the Amygdala. Thus fear can return again and again and while often beneficial to man, can also be detrimental until our trust in God gives us the ability to over-ride that fear when necessary. The good news is that the Amygdala can be re-trained to process our memories/experiences differently and thereby allow us to by-pass or overcome the sensation of fear from any particular event. This "overcoming" process is representative of the brain's ability to re-categorize our experiences by separating those which we once thought were "bad" from those which we realize can no longer bring us harm.

Sometimes however we can be overcome by fear and suffer from panic attacks. This is because we rely totally on the Amygdala and have not accumulated the tools with which we can reason the fear away through the neo-cortex. Thus Satan can use this natural response against us unless we are supported and encouraged by our faith in God. It is our *lack of knowledge*, our lack of experience, our lack of understanding which allows the brain to send the wrong signals to our body rather than use the knowledge which God provides to help us. This is why panic attacks are prevalent. The Bible tells us that lacking information can destroy our faith in God and only the knowledge which scripture provides can help us as God's Plan of Salvation moves forward; moves into its next phase and its era of completion.

Fear can also arise when our belief systems appear to be under attack. Few of us like change, few realize that there may be more to God's plan than we could ever imagine. Few want to even consider what may have been accomplished by our Heavenly Father during a different era such as the great Mayan civilization, or the eons before the creation of time such as the era when evolution wrought its changes on our world. Most Christians desire their belief systems to be tied into a neat little bundle which does not allow for new information or incredible activities outside of the coming of Christ.

However, the true Christian who has complete trust in God can handle the unveiling of new information. Their willingness to learn allows them to consider a concept which is different than they'd originally thought. A true and trusting Christian must be willing to explore what scripture can tell us and not what Satan tells us about these different eras of the past and the future. The miracle and mystery of scripture is that these questions are answered as mankind evolves to a point where they can and will trust in a greater God and more complex universe than they'd first imagined.

We short change God by limiting what we want our "faith" to include, what we *expect* God to be and to do. We short change ourselves when we believe what Satan has instilled in our heart rather than what God tells us in scripture. There is so much more to God's Plan of Salvation than we can fathom, and such perfect love, perfect thought and perfect righteousness behind God's plan that we will always find ourselves amazed and our faith strengthened if we can continue to trust.

We have much to learn about God and His incredible Plan for mankind, and about the power of

Satan and why God invested in such an intricate plan to destroy evil. And....why mankind could be of such importance to Him. The belief that soon Satan will forever be prevented from harming the children of God helps us endure what we live through, what we learn, and what it will take for us to truly trust God. Our goal is to overcome the fears which Satan places in our hearts regarding the many facets of God's Plan of Salvation and His protection.

But as we wait for God's plan to be completed, we must understand that Satan can influence the thoughts and belief systems of ordinary, even god-fearing, people. Satan has the power to blind the hearts and minds of men and to confuse their thought process. It is through this confusion that Satan creates the doubt which can take hold of our faith and bring a very difficult and ungodly challenge to our future.

It is to circumvent this doubt that God asks us to learn His words. It is through scripture that we learn how the various situations of the world can be explained. But it is also through scripture that we learn of what is to come and why God has so lovingly and patiently provided for us through such varying venues. It is because of God's loving nature, His all knowing and all seeing capabilities that questions can be answered and doubt and fear allayed about the times in which we live, the times before life as we know it, and the times to come. It is through scripture that God gives us what we need so we will not be afraid. Knowledge is the key to building and maintaining the faith which will allow us to overcome our fears, to learn of God's plan and trust Him.....especially as the final phase of God's plan begins to unfold.

God sees every circumstance, and every heart's attitude, and knows how Satan works his deceit to capture our souls and break our faith. Thus God has given us what we need when we need it. He has clearly explained that His words in the scriptures are a mystery, are hidden explanations which He opens to those who, with a pure heart, seek to find them and does so at just the right time. Scripture tells us that God's words will act as an awakening to many who desire to increase their faith and maintain their journey to God's new kingdom. Scripture also tells us that the meaning of the words God provides is **_not_** unveiled to those who doubt, or those who seek to use scripture to disprove our Heavenly Father's plan of salvation.

Scripture tells us that God desires that **all** men be saved but that there will be those who will be lost because of their free will; their personal decision to maintain their lack of knowledge, **_their unwillingness to open their hearts and minds to God and strive to meet the criteria which He requires from those He wants to bring into His new kingdom._** God often refers to this attitude as being "hard-hearted". But for those who do seek, who do believe, who do desire to develop a deep, unshakable child-like faith, we must understand that the next phase of our learning experience will show us that God is so much more than we had ever imagined.

It will demonstrate that our Heavenly Father is all in all, that he controls the entire Universe and has controlled all things throughout the ages, throughout the eons of time which we cannot begin to….. or are willing to….imagine. Despite our childishness, God has given us the power to find the answer through prayer and scripture if we have an open mind, are willing to trust Him, and with a pure heart ask Him to open our understanding. We must desire that God will instill in us that which we need.

As new information and new technologies unfold, as the world slips into the world of terror, of new discoveries about our ancestors, and offers the de-classification of old discoveries, we will be called upon to learn, to be patient, to have an open mind, but most of all to trust. No matter how unique the situation appears, God has followed a specific plan meant for the good and godly furtherance of mankind and will create a blessing from the circumstances which have and will unfold. Thus our willingness to learn, to trust and to accept God's immense plan for mankind and the elimination of evil are three attributes we must endeavor to acquire. This requires a working knowledge of scripture, a personal victory over our Adam-like nature of fear and doubt, and a child-like faith in our Heavenly Father. These attributes also help us discern the lies and deceit Satan brings us.

As we live through evil circumstances or we acquire chilling, potentially faith shattering new information, we will be called upon to exercise a new kind of faith; one which encompasses eons of time and many approaches to bring mankind to God, to shatter evil for all eternity. We may balk at some of this information. We may want God to manifest Himself so clearly that we could instantly banish all doubt and fear; banish every anxiety and understand with clarity how God has directed His plan and used His power.

Surely our Heavenly Father wishes that He could show us how closely affiliated with our circumstances He is, but if He did, He would not be fulfilling the law of righteousness under which He has chosen to labour. Without God's adherence to the laws of righteousness, Satan could accuse Him of affecting man's free will to choose between good and evil, to choose to trust God no matter what we face or what we learn. And it is this choice which every individual must personally make which deems us worthy for the new kingdom God plans for the joy of all who are righteous.

Therefore, in every difficult circumstance we must demonstrate that we freely choose to handle our journey in a godly manner and freely choose to continue to trust our Heavenly Father. We must use our personal free will to decide how we want to handle our new challenges, and through that choice grow in faith as we dedicate ourselves to God's will. Second guessing God and why He did things as He did is not placing our trust in His will, in His decisions. But when we do, it allows God to further manifest His love and power by blessing and protecting us. Acknowledging our past blessings and openly identifying them as the godly interventions they are touches God's heart and tells Him that we love Him.

However when we do not acknowledge what God has done for us we may fall into a greater fear and entertain more anxiety when we face our new challenges. Fear and doubt can then override our faith and allow Satan to harm us and to destroy our entire and currently limited concept of God and His plan of Salvation. When we entertain doubt about God's plan, then Satan has accomplished what he set out to do. But when we increase our faith, nothing can shake our belief that God loves us and that His plan is and has always been for the good of mankind, and we can rest in the perfection of God's righteousness and the wonder of His love through which He will eliminate evil forever.

If we look back on our past difficulties with this in mind, we will recognize a pattern through which our lives were shaped and our paths directed. We will see that even our *negative* experiences and *painful* associations helped frame our way of thinking and readied us to further open our understanding. We will see that these experiences taught us the value of spurning the temptations of evil and making the decision to live according to God's statutes….and to TRUST God implicitly!

As we look for and appreciate the blessings gleaned from our past experiences, our hearts open to God. This action spiritually invites Him to work in our soul to help us recognize His love and trust in His plan for mankind. It helps us make the changes needed to become a part of the Bride of Christ and to obey God. We begin to accept and believe that God will turn even what we might see as devastating circumstances into a blessing which will help us weather our challenges with greater courage.

This process of total trust however, does not occur overnight. It is a slow process, a learning process where we make the personal decision to believe and obey. These exercises are but one rung of the ladder of human growth and understanding. Our future calls for us to enter a new phase where *more will be required* of us. We will be called upon to look at scripture in a different light and to uncover the mysteries it holds allowing that information to manifest into an even greater trust in God and a greater understanding of the immenseness of His plan of salvation. As we recount when, where, and how God has blessed us in the past, we develop the ability to trust Him more fully with our future.

But why has God addressed fear so often throughout scripture? Why is God concerned that this emotion could destroy our faith? What are the fears we have had or will have which requires so much re-assurance? Is God simply addressing our everyday concerns or is there something yet to come which is far greater? Could it be that as we look at history and digest some of the information which pertains to ancient civilizations our original belief system could be shaken? Will we still believe? Will we be willing to accept that God's plan is, was and will be what is right for us?

Could it be that we will be faced with many new questions about our faith, about Christ, about the life Christ lived and what He brought to mankind? Will we wonder why Christ came when He did.... and why He was not sent to those earlier civilizations which appeared so advanced in their technology. Will new information and new technology make us wonder what is true and what is not? Will it be through scripture that we can glean the answers to these questions and begin to gain a deeper understanding of the immenseness of God? Will we be able to recognize that God's love and concern for us was why God's plan has covered eons of time in teaching mankind what they need to know?

Could it be that filling in these gaps via the words in scripture prepares us for what is to come and helps build the trust which is and will be needed to move to the final phase of God's plan for mankind? Is the separation of good and evil for all eternity worth such an enormous effort? Are we? Perhaps all that we have yet to learn will not diminish our faith but strengthen it. Perhaps no matter what non-believers say; no matter what new information comes to light, we are being given the tools through which our faith can become unshakable as God's Plan of Salvation moves into its final phase.

I hope that this first chapter sets the stage for understanding fear, for understanding why our lack of knowledge creates that fear, and where we might go from here. I hope to demonstrate that there have been phases to God's plan for mankind which we now need to explore and trust. We may wonder about the phase of God's plan which covered the span of time when there was no Sun or moon or stars to create time as we know it…. thus allowed for evolution. We may wonder why ancient civilizations worshipped differently than we do. But as we explore what scripture tells us which might explain this phenomenon, we will be filled with wonder.

As we examine the phases of God's plan for mankind and begin to see that scripture addressed so much more than we realized we begin to understand what God means about scripture being a mystery. As God moves into His new phase and opens more of the mystery of scripture to us, we will be fascinated to learn why earlier civilizations worshipped the deities they did and why God chose to introduce His power in such a manner. We will see why the gift of Christ prepared us for the development of a faith so strong and a love so sure and so deep that we would understand God and the immensity of His plan and trust what was and what is yet to come.

I hope to describe a new phase which might be on the horizon for us which will challenge our faith and show us why God has addressed fear in such detail. I hope to demonstrate God's infinite overview of the Universe as He completes His plan to destroy evil and create in mankind a Bride for His Son.

God does not open every mystery of Scripture to mankind until the proper moment. God waits until mankind is ready for such revelations. God gives us an understanding of His words as we are ready to accept them. This speaks of God's concern for us and His compassion for us as little children still in the learning phase of life. It tells us that despite the evil we see in this world, God loves us, is patient with us, understands our weakness, sees and responds to our needs, and is right beside us as we walk even through the valley of death!

I hope that as we consider the possibility of even more astonishing phases in God's Plan of Salvation, our faith will not diminish but increase and prove our worth as children of God. I hope that together we can mature in faith and wisdom to become the adult God desires as a bride for His Son. When we seek understanding, when we desire to learn so we can serve God with all our heart and all our mind and let Him know how much we love Him, God will help us find everything we need!

HELEN GLOWACKI

Chapter Two

THE ENORMITY OF TIME

As we asked in the previous chapter, why did God make so many provisions for us to deal with the emotion of fear? Could it be that He is concerned about new revelations or questions which might arise which could attack our belief system? Is God preparing us for the entire scope of what He has done thus far, or for what He plans to do in the future to ensure our protection from Satan? Certainly we recognize that faith and Biblical values have decreased and unbelief, hatred and envy have increased in the world in which we live. Some churches are half empty, a "New Age" religion has emerged, political parties cannot compromise, and atheists are succeeding in removing faith-related words, symbols and icons from our schools and government.

But out of this hatred and divide, millions of people from every walk of life and from every area of our country have arisen who now voice their desire to bring Biblical principles *back* into their lives, *back* into the schools, and *back* into their country. They now recognize that for the last 50 – 60 years there has been an assault on our country's Judeo/Christian beliefs and principles, and as a result, our culture has suffered.

However, many are now being drawn once again to studying the Bible and inserting God's statutes into their lives. Historians are being inspired to re-discover scripture as a key to better understanding both past and future events from a Biblical point of view. And others are being brought testimony to open their eyes to the fact that they may not become a part of God's new kingdom without making changes in their lives.

Many parents are taking a closer look at what schools are teaching their children, and have been surprised by what they have found......and not found..... in their children's textbooks. Parents are questioning what is being omitted in their children's education and what is being taught which is not conducive to a godly life. Parents are asking why their children's school curriculum accommodates a more liberal and less godly narrative. Seeking answers to these questions, and developing a goal to reclaim Biblical values and a more godly direction for their school systems, parents are discovering that our founding fathers *expected* textbooks to teach Biblical principles, to teach that God is our benefactor and protector, and to teach that our Constitution was inspired by God. Many are learning that God will hold them responsible if they do not teach their children about God.

Solomon wrote that parents are to: *"Train up a child in the way he should go, and when he is old he will not depart from it."* (Proverbs 22:6)

Through this, parents are gaining the confidence to work toward correction and change. They are demanding a more rounded education for their children.... not one which directs young minds toward a path which negates godly instruction. Parents are fighting back to restore what has been removed and changed to influence their children's way of thinking through a more liberal experience.

For years, schools have taught the Theory of Evolution while completely eliminating any reference to the "Theory" of Creation. Now, however there is a movement to learn why the Theory of Evolution is a subject which was given carte blanche in the classroom while the Creation has been banned. Parents want to change that way of thinking and encourage children to learn both views and learn that they are indeed compatible! According to scripture, evolution and creation do co-exist and this needs to be taught to fully demonstrate that God is in control of all things.

Our founding fathers used scripture in almost all their speeches. They openly praised God for what He provided for them. They built our Constitution around Biblical principles. They honored our flag and both taught and practiced patriotism. In times past children saluted the flag, recited the Pledge of Allegiance and bowed their head for a moment of silent prayer. Now, little of that remains in our schools because of a few atheists who labored to block these activities. Parents want to bring these statements of faith and patriotism back into the education system.

Scripture is a mix of the past, the present, and the future and provides more information than first meets the eye. While scripture contains the formula by which God asks us to live and is the mechanism used to describe His Plan of Salvation for mankind, it also contains pockets of information which amazingly describe the heavens and the universe which no man had seen when scripture was written.

Few know that scripture addresses the loyalties we should have to government, how to choose our leaders and what attributes we should demand in them. Exodus 18:21 teaches, *"Moreover thou shalt provide out of all the people able* **men, such as fear God, men of truth**, *hating covetousness; and place such over them to be rulers of thousands, and rulers of hundreds, rulers of fifties, andrulers of ten."* This clearly tells us to support and vote for those who value truth and who fear (worship) God.

11 Chronicles 19:5-7 tells us, *"And he set judges in the land throughout all the fenced cities of Judah, city by city. And said to the judges, Take heed what ye do; for ye judge not for man, but for the Lord, who is with you in judgment. Wherefore now let the fear of the Lord be upon you; take heed and do it: for there is no iniquity with the Lord our God, nor respect of persons, nor taking of gifts."* Here a warning is clearly issued to those who govern. They

are told to fear (worship) God and govern according to His will.

11 Chronicles 19:10 adds, *"....between law and commandments, statutes and judgments, ye shall even warn them that they trespass not against the Lord, and so wrath will come upon you, and upon your brethren; this do, and ye shall not trespass."* Here scripture tells us that where governing occurs, no trespass upon God must occur and that "ye" shall warn them about this admonition or we will all suffer God's wrath.

Psalms 9:16-17 warns, *"The Lord is known by the judgment which he executeth; the wicked is ensnared in the work of his own hands....**The wicked** shall be turned into hell, **and all the nations** that forget God."* Here we are warned that we will be ensnared by our allowing evil lawmakers to govern, and that our nation will suffer when we come under the rule of wicked lawmakers. Further, that if we forget God, as a nation we may face hell and as individuals we may lose our soul salvation.

11 Chronicles 7:14 comforts us with the words, *"If my people, which are called by my name, shall humble themselves, and pray, and seek my face, and turn from their wicked ways; then will I hear from heaven, and will forgive their sin, and **will heal their land.***" Clearly God is offering us a second chance to stop the wickedness and turn back to Him. If we add works to our faith to accomplish this, He will heal our nation.

Malachi 2:8 acknowledges, *"But ye are departed out of the way; **ye have caused** many to stumble at the law; **ye have corrupted** the covenant of Levi, sayeth the Lord of hosts."* Christians have clearly departed from God by allowing, even encouraging the corruption of government to occur,and have, by their inaction, allowed it to continue. God notices those who have been corrupt and who cause our nation and their people to stumble.

Matthew 18:6 warns, *"But whoso shall offend one of these little ones which believe in me, it were better for him that a millstone were hanged around* *his neck, and that he drowned in the depth of the sea. "*This scripture clearly warns those who are responsible for harming God's children in word or deed and warns that they will be held accountable. This could include removing God, prayer, and the Biblical principles upon which this nation was founded from the schools and textbooks of our children and even the banning of Nativity sets, crosses and the words "In God We Trust" on our currency.

Malachi 2:17 warns, *"Ye have wearied the Lord with your words.....When you say, Every one that doeth evil is good in the sight of the Lord, and he delighteth in them; or Where is the God of judgment?"* Here God acknowledges that we are complaining about our situation. He clearly tells us that our complaining wearies Him and will be of no avail because **we ourselves** are the cause of allowing our Biblical principles to be lost. Over and over God comes to every individual to knock on their heart's door and still few let Him in; few decide to live their life as God asks.

In terms of how we should vote and what kind of a political system we should support, these are just a few verses from scripture which address the governing of the people. In every verse, God warns that His principles and His might must always be respected. Thus scripture is acknowledged as an incredible and godly resource for mankind not only spiritually but also through the governing body and personal lives of those they elect.

As we seek to learn what God tells us through scripture and move into the question of how evolution can be reconciled with the creation we must discern what it is that we must first seek. One question we must ask is what created our current concept of time. Evolution defies time as we know it because carbon dating encompasses possibly billions of years in the kind of "time" we understand. Thus it is important for us to understand the concept of time and how that concept has placed us in a particular era. It is important that we ask what God did which moved the creation from the eons of the past where there was no time as we know it, into what we experience today as a repetitive twenty-four-hour day.

As we try to understand how time exists as we currently experience it, we need to look at what might be required to create or encompass time. As we examine scripture and the process God followed to create the world, we learn that it is the creation of the sun which gave us time as we experience it today. Simply put, the answer lies in *the relationship* between the earth and the sun. It is the speed and manner in which the earth revolves around its axis as it revolves around the sun which creates the day and the night. For us this occurs every twenty-four hours.

The twenty-four hours it takes the earth to make one turn on its axis determines the length of time that one day and one night offers us. We can concede that God Himself created and directed the speed and manner in which the earth moves around the sun thus determined what time would entail as we would be experiencing it.

God's control of all the heavenly bodies is referenced many times in scripture and a particular reference to the sun is found in Job 9:7 where Job asks *"Who shakes the earth out of its place and its pillars tremble; who commands the sun not to shine?"* And Joshua 10:11-13 states: *"So the sun stood still until the nation avenged themselves of their enemies......and (the sun) hasted not to go down about a whole day."*

We are told in 2 Kings 20:9-11 *"Then Isaiah said 'This is the sign to you from the Lord that the shadow go forward 10 degrees or go backward 10 degrees....and (the Lord) brought the shadow 10 degrees backward by which it had gone down on the sun dial of Ahaz."*

Further supporting evidence is found in the history of other cultures such as the New Zealand Maori people who have a myth about how their hero Maui *stopped* the sun. The Mexican annals of the Cuahtitian's also document a night which continued for an extended time.

Interestingly, the Amorites who Joshua was fighting when God made the Sun stand still to give him the victory, were sun and moon worshippers thus for them to have to succumb to the God of Israel represented by Joshua was a devastating and faith shattering experience. God may have chosen to work with this particular phenomenon because of the deities worshipped by the Amorites.

As we study the phenomenon of time, we also learn that when the part of the planet we personally occupy is facing the sun, it is daylight, and when the earth rotates so we are not facing the sun, it is nighttime. In further explanation science teaches us that the earth moves in a sort of egg-shaped or elliptic orbit around the sun, yet its axis always remains tilted in the same direction relative to the plane of the orbit. This tilt causes the sun's rays to strike each part of the earth at various angles throughout the orbit.

The angle that the sun's rays hit the earth and the distance of the earth from the sun causes the seasons. One full orbit around the sun brings the earth back to the starting point and the amount of time required for this leads to our concept of the year.

This, together with the rotation of the earth on its axis which causes our night and day, **gives us our current concept of time.** These facts are **indisputable** studies from scientific reports and fully support why time is calculated as it is today.

Without the earth's rotations around its axis and around the sun as they are now, we might have a twenty-eight-hour day, or always be cold or always be warm. Thus, the angle of the earth to the sun, how far it is from the sun, whether it faces toward or away from the sun, and how fast it spins on its axis, determines our days and nights, our seasons, and our time.

Looking for an explanation about how evolution can exist side by side with the creation, we can find some fascinating material in the Book of Genesis which tells the story of how the world was created. Scripture tells us that it took seven days to create the world, but actually it took six days to create because on the seventh day, God rested.

Carbon dating is the cause of the conflict about the compatibility of evolution with creation. Carbon dating demonstrates that the earth is billions of years old while creationists have often insisted that scripture demonstrates a much younger earth. However, **scripture clearly reconciles these two views** making each wrong if they negate the other and the two theories compatible.

Sadly, much of the conflict about how evolution fits into what the Bible tells us relies on the fact that "days", as we know them, are made up of a period of twenty-four hours each and exists only because of the relationship between the earth and the sun. However, if we look carefully at the word "days", scripture itself gives us an incredible clue about how carbon dating, along with some parts of evolution, is compatible with creation. Scripture clearly demonstrates how the two apparently contradictory theories, creation and evolution, are, instead quite compatible.

When we read the first verse in Genesis and then follow this accounting from the first verse to the nineteenth verse, we find that the sun and moon and **the 'seasons, days, and years' were not created until the *fourth* day.** This is fascinating information because without the sun and the moon in existence we could not experience the era of time as we know it today. Therefore, we can conclude that ***it wasn't until this fourth day that we could have entered into a 24 hour day*** or time in general, as we now experience it.

We can read the exact words which describe this new era about the creation of the sun and moon in Genesis 1:14, 16 and 19. These verses tell us: *"And God said, Let there be lights in the firmament of the heaven to divide the day from the night, and let them be for signs, and for seasons, and for days, and years." "And God made two great lights; the greater light to rule the day, and the lesser light to rule the night; he made stars also." "And the evening and the morning were the fourth day."*

Thus the first four "days", or two thirds of the time it took God to produce our world, are not days as we know them because time, as we now experience it, was not yet introduced into the Creation. Psalm 90:4 in the Holy Bible gives us a hint about time during these first "days": *"For a thousand years in thy sight are but as yesterday when it is past, and as a watch in the night."*

2 Peter 3:8 states, *"But, beloved, be not ignorant of this one thing, that one day is with the Lord as a thousand years, and a thousand years as one day."* It is important to note that in this verse we read the word "as" rather than the word "are" meaning that there is a ***similarity***, not an actuality, of one day and one thousand years.

As we seek to understand what scripture tells us about the era of evolution and we read verses 1 through 13 in Genesis Chapter 1, we recognize that these verses do not correspond to time as we know it in the Creation. Scripture explains that without the constraints of time, an evolutionary process could very well have occurred.

Many of the years relative to carbon dating may fall into this period described in scripture which existed before the completion of the fourth day. Verses 1 through 13 speak of the form, the darkness, the waters, light and darkness, the firmament, and finally the division between dry land and the seas. All of these elements then were a part of the evolutionary construct.

Genesis 1:9 and 10 says, *"And God said, Let the waters under the heaven be gathered together unto one place, and let the dry land appear: and it was so. And God called the dry land Earth; and the gathering together of the waters called the Seas: and God saw that it was good."* These building blocks in the evolutionary process occurred on the *third* "day", one "day" *before* the sun and moon, days and nights, and seasons were established, and **before time as we know it was established.**

This tells us that many thousands even tens of thousands of years could have gone into the evolutionary process up to the end of the fourth "day" when God completed the sun and moon for the earth. It was only then that the seasons, days, and years as we experience them were created. What the Bible says indicates that creation and evolution are more compatible than we first recognized. This means that carbon dating and many parts of the process of evolution which has been derived from carbon dating seem fully compatible with scripture. In fact, carbon dating **supports** the relationship scripture describes of evolution and creation rather than disproves it even if the years calculated by carbon dating are not totally or precisely accurate.

Interestingly, as we view what scripture tells us from this different point of view and read of God's work on the fifth day as described in Genesis 1:24

we learn even more. *"Let the earth bring forth the living creature after his own kind."* What these words seem to indicate is that because of the limits to time which have just been established via the previous verses, **no longer would these creatures change through the process of evolution** into new species; they would instead bring forth only other creatures just like themselves. This fact further establishes the differences which occurred once time as we know it came into existence.

As we wonder why this debate between evolutionists and creationists still exists we can again look to the Bible for the answer. By reading about the encounter between Eve and the serpent in the Garden of Eden, and subsequent encounters between man and evil, we recognize that according to the Bible, mankind has an enemy who wishes to separate man from God. Thus, the debate between the evolutionist and the creationist is important to Satan as he very much wants to prevent man from accepting scripture as truth.

Satan works hard to encourage unbelievers to denounce the fact that creation and evolution can co-exist. Satan realizes that if he does not discourage a belief in scripture, more men might believe in God simply because they would recognize the amazing accuracy and forethought found in the Bible. Additionally, our concept of time appears to be addressed in Mark 13:20, where we read: *"......... And except that the Lord had shortened those days, no flesh should be saved: but for the elect's sake, whom he hath chosen, he **hath shortened the days.**"* It is interesting to consider the words 'hath shortened'. If we interpret this to mean that God had *already* shortened the days and that He did this when He created our sun and moon on that fourth day, this would give even more credence to the argument that **days, <u>before the sun and moon existed,</u> could very well have been much longer**.

Revelation 10:6 says, *"And I sware by him that liveth for ever and ever, who created heaven, and the things that therein are, and the earth, and the things that therein are, and the sea, and the things which are therein, that there should be time no longer."* The words '**there should be time no longer**' indicate that we will live without the confinement of time as we know it when God's Plan of Salvation is complete and God creates the new heaven and the new earth. This further indicates that God controls time and that time as we know it might have been created just for us and for a specific span of time. Joshua 10:13–14 tells us, *"And the sun stood still, and the moon stayed………" "…… So the sun stood still in the midst of heaven, and hasted not to go down about a whole day. And there was no day like that before it or after it."* Here is another indication that God controls time. This is another example of the myriad of information scripture provides and then backs up by providing additional verses in other areas of scripture which support the miracle and mystery of the information it provides!

Scientists claim that our universe is made up of dark matter that contains a kind of web which connects multitudes of superclusters, which themselves are made up of about one hundred billion galaxies. We live in the Mergo cluster in the relatively small Milky Way galaxy, which contains one hundred billion stars, one of which is our sun.

Interestingly, in the beginning of Genesis, *before* God created our sun and moon and thus provided time **as we know it**, the words firmament, void, waters, darkness, and light are used. Webster's dictionary says that the word "firmament" means the vault or arch of the sky and also means a 'support.' The word void could be the dark matter itself, and the word firmament could refer to the webs within the dark matter which hold together the superclusters of galaxies.

When some challenge that man and not God wrote the Bible they are stating that men did so without the help of God. Thus to them, scripture cannot be trusted. However, it is interesting to ask how mere man could have made reference to our galaxy or to what existed in the heavens at the time when the

Bible was written? We need to ask the naysayers how could any man have known what a firmament was, what it did, and how it worked? How could mere man in his limited knowledge of the world, especially at that time...provide so much scientific information in the words he wrote unless those words were inspired by God? Most of what we can uncover about the Creation only God could know, yet throughout scripture we find reference after reference to the universe. Those references were far beyond mankind's understanding of the world when scripture was written. Biblical scholars therefore acclaim that the words of scripture were inspired by God; by the Holy Spirit working within the heart and soul of the authors of scripture. Certainly this appears to be the case as we read the early chapters of Genesis.

Darkness, according to the Webster's Dictionary means devoid of light, not reflecting, receiving, transmitting, or radiating light, and could be what existed before the stars were created. One of the definitions of the word light says it is an electromagnetic radiation in the wavelength range including infrared, visible, ultraviolet, and X-rays traveling in a vacuum with a speed of about 186,281 miles per second. If Biblically this refers to stars it would support the big bang theory which Christians believe was *a controlled event with an engineered result,* not a haphazard event with an unpredictable result. In other words....fully controlled by God!

All of this information demonstrates that scripture does provide a myriad of information both to reassure man of God's existence and to prepare him for what will be required of him to become a part of the new world God will create for mankind. Our Heavenly Father clearly tells us that He will create a new world; a new heaven and earth for His children. It will be a world of no sorrow, no tears, no sickness...a world of no evil. It will emanate a love so pure that there is no need for a sun to light our path.

As we read about what God plans for our future, and read what has occurred in the past to move the development of mankind along, we can see that the Bible offers us so much. As we carefully examine scripture we learn that it is filled with mystery, filled with information just waiting to be unveiled. We also recognize that scripture is layered and awaiting our ability to understand what God wants us to know. Scripture is a gift to mankind. It is to help us navigate what is almost too difficult for us to comprehend in our present state.

Therefore, in conclusion to our discussion about evolution and creation and how scripture has so easily joined these two components for us, we can see how we may have worried unnecessarily over the arguments found in these discussions. Perhaps God had concerns over the fear man would experience from this information and saw that some could lose their faith over the dispute. Perhaps this is why God included the answers to our questions in scripture. Learning that God inspired the writers of scripture to include such information about evolution and creation is mind boggling! It demonstrates how a discovery such as carbon dating need not destroy our faith, and encourages us to move on to yet another interesting discovery of the way in which God is preparing a wonderful future for us.

Perhaps we are entering an era of new discoveries, demanding a new set of questions and a new experience. We may be ready to unveil some of the circumstances of our past so we can understand that which was not unveiled to us earlier. We might even ask why didn't God provide earlier civilizations with the gift of Christ and the wonder of grace? Why did God choose to send Christ to us and not to earlier civilizations? How did the people living in those earlier and remote civilizations understand the engineering techniques required to build pyramids and align their buildings to the stars?

Why do the hieroglyphics of these earlier civilizations represent "gods" of great power but seemingly have no connection to our own belief system? What did God accomplish through and with these people?   Will the answers to these questions destroy our faith and cause us the fear which God addresses throughout scripture?   Or will they help us see a much bigger picture of God's magnificence and all encompassing power?

Will any of this information help us make that most important decision to learn of God and then follow his instructions?   Will our fortitude to give our lives to God be strengthened?   Will we recognize that God reaches out to us every day whether through a book, a person, a TV show, a radio show, a magazine, an experience of faith, scripture, or a myriad of other venues?   Will we make a renewed effort to know God *as He wants us to know Him*.....or still remain complacent?

Chapter Three

ANCIENT CIVILATIONS

Peppered across the entire world are remnants of ancient civilizations whose people worshipped various gods depicted in their hieroglyphics as coming from the skies. Scientists have determined that these "gods" taught the people the incredible technologies they appeared to have utilized to build pyramids and to interpret the movement of the stars.

It is amazing to note that pyramids are found in so many different areas of the world and are very similar to one another. This hints at the possibility that the "gods" of these ancient people were capable of great intellect, could travel anywhere they desired, at great speed and visit every area of our world.

Few people have recognized that pyramids, all very similar to one another, have been found in Egypt, Mexico, Mesopotamia, Sudan, Nigeria, Greece, Spain, China, MesoAmerica, North America, the Roman Empire, Europe, India, Indonesia, and Peru. One pyramid in Egypt apparently dates all the way back to 2700 BC.

When researching ancient civilizations we find that almost every part of the world lists such a civilization and that these people worshipped many different deities from animals to clay figures to the sun and the stars and many things found in nature. Thus it makes us wonder about God's involvement in these people's lives and why He appears to have gifted these civilizations such great technology but not an understanding of the One God? We then ask if these people will be a part of God's new world and exactly who were the gods they worshipped?

Perhaps scripture explains this too when it describes what went on in Heaven during the time when these ancient civilizations existed and before Christianity was introduced. Perhaps as scripture says, *"There is a time for everything"*, as explanation that that God's Plan of Salvation included this era purposefully. In fact Ecclesiastes 3:1-8 tells us: *"For everything there is an appointed time, and an appropriate time for every activity on earth: A time to be born, and a time to die; a time to plant, and a time to uproot what was planted; A time to kill, and a time to heal; a time to break down, and a time to build up; A time to weep, and a time to laugh; a time to mourn, and a time to dance. A time to throw away stones, and a time to gather stones; a time to embrace, and a time to refrain from embracing; A time to search, and a time to give something up as lost; a time to keep, and a time to throw away; A time to rip, and a time to sew; a time to keep silent, and a time to speak. A time to love, and a time to hate; a time for war, and a time for peace.* "Perhaps God was not yet ready to launch His interventions on earth but was preparing in heaven what was first needed.

During this time period, was God busy creating the angels and positioning the heavenly hierarchy which would look after or govern the creation of man who would follow God and accept His rule over them? Was the time of "evolution" not only for the earth but also for the heavens and for God's plan to come to fruition?

Surely our God, who is omnipotent and omnipresent, would have foreseen the evil He would eventually have to eliminate. Surely "time" for God did not exist to limit His long term vision.

Nevertheless, scripture does give us a glimpse into the early part of God's plan as we read that before He created man, God created the angels and also created Satan who was originally named Lucifer.

Lucifer was an archangel and God elevated him to a position where he would sit at one side of God's throne while Christ would sit on the other. Scripture tells us that Lucifer became jealous of Christ and of God's apparent favor toward Christ and from Satan's jealousy the enmity and hate now so prevalent in our world began. Perhaps this was an era which had to occur before the rest of God's plan for a perfect world of love could be initiated.

Scripture also refers to the "giants" which walked the earth before Adam and Eve were introduced to the Garden of Eden. Were these the remnants of earlier civilizations or perhaps even the "gods" brought from the heavens to guide earlier civilizations toward a better life? Or were they the fallen angels cast from heaven for their rebellion?

Again we have questions which go unanswered while we are given some insight into a God and a plan so much greater than we'd originally understood. None of this information nor the questions this information raises really affects the promises we have been given for our future. They simply make us expand our view of all that God did in a world which moved through a greater evolutionary period than we originally understood.

Perhaps the "visitors" to these ancient civilization were angels sent to help these people survive and to show them a universe so much greater than they could envision. Perhaps worshipping heavenly deities were a precursor for the development of one worshipping the true Creator.

We may not like this idea, but there could be an important reason for these mores to exist which has not yet been revealed to us. From the Incas of Ecuador, Peru and Chili who worshipped the Sun God "Inti" to the Aztecs and Mayans whose pyramids were larger than those found in Egypt, to the Persians, Greeks, Romans, Chinese, and Indus Valley civilizations and more, each are found to have developed the desire to worship a god.

Was this how faith came into being and God patiently waited for and prepared for the next step in the growth and development of mankind?

Clay figures from civilizations such as the Hattians in Turkey, The Zapotecs in Mesopotamia, The Vinca in Serbia and Romania, The Hurrian in Mesopotamia, The Punt in South America, The Norte Chico in Peru, The Elamites in Iran, The Dilmum in Bahrain, and The Harrappan (Indus Valley) in Pakistan all demonstrate that rules or mores were developed for their people to follow in order to pay homage for their blessings.

If indeed there was a leap from ape to man, worship and appreciation would been quite a feat to accomplish.   If instead, the people of these civilizations were "planted" by a "god" from heaven, they would have had to learn how to act within a closed society perhaps through the rules and regulations put forth by a religious system.

Could this painstakingly slow move toward a godly society have been God's plan all along? But if so why did these societies die out. Where did they go? Why doesn't scripture mention what happened to them? Why did "giants" exist outside the Garden of Eden when God created Adam and Eve?

All of this conjecture could easily break our faith and cause the fear in our hearts to mount. Those moved by these questions may be unable to accept a change in their initial perception of God's plan and be prevented from accepting what might yet come. Do we need this information to fully trust God's Plan of Salvation as we face the future?

Perhaps the declassification of materials pertaining to UFO's can be reconciled with our faith. Perhaps what we learn from the ancient civilizations will instill in us an understanding which will prevent today's discoveries from shaking our faith. Could this have been God's purpose?

Could the Mayans claim that their nine major "gods" were the creators and formers of human life fit in with what scripture tells us of the work of God's angels?

Few people are aware of the duties and diversity of the angels. Few know that scripture tells us of the three levels of Heaven in which reside three different types of angels each with a different task. Few realize that it is in the lower part of heaven where angels, archangels and principalities reside and that these are the three types of angels who usually communicate directly with mankind.

We can learn from scripture that the angels which are called the Cherubim, the Seraphim and the Thrones provide **counsel** and live in the third or upper part of heaven. Those called the Dominions, the Virtues and the Powers, **govern,** and reside in the middle heaven. Those called the Principalities, the Archangels and the Angels, act as **messengers** and live in that part of heaven closest to earth.

Were the angels the "gods" of ancient civilizations? Or were those gods the fallen angels who were sent to earth with Lucifer when they were banished from the heavens? Scripture tells us that the fallen angels who joined Lucifer's rebellion against God had resided in the second and third spheres of heaven, each holding ranks of those who lived in that sphere, thus able to perform the works they were created to perform.

As we read of the cruel practices of some of these ancient civilizations we may think that they surely were satanic; were in fact evil and demonic. This might indicate that these people were misled by **_fallen_** angels and became evil in nature thereby could have filled with earth with evil.

Revelation 9:11 tells us that the demons or fallen angels have a king named "the angel of the abyss" (bottomless pit) or "Abaddon". This name in Hebrew means "Destroyer". Abaddon is also referred to as Apollyon (the Greek word for destroyer), and as the "Beast".

Scripture warns that before Christ returns there will be a massive *"falling away"* of religion (11 Thessalonians 2:1) because of the works of a *"man of sin"*(verse 3). From 11 Thessalonians 2:6 we learn that the *"mystery of lawlessness"* will be in effect at this time. Scripture explains that when the fifth angel blows his trumpet as God completes His Plan of Salvation, an angel comes to earth with a key to unlock the Abyss (bottomless pit) and brings with him a great chain with which he will imprison Satan in the Abyss for the duration of the Millennium or Thousand Year Kingdom of Peace. (Revelation 20:1-3)

Revelation 17:4 speaks of "Babylon the Great", the false religious governmental system of Satan which will rule the earth for three and one half years, forty two months, or twelve hundred and sixty days, according to scripture. (Scripture records this period of time in these three ways.) (Revelation 13:5, Revelation 11:3, Daniel 7:25, Daniel 12:7)

This is a time when those in power will denigrate God, speak blasphemy against God, against His tabernacles, His Holy City, against those who dwell in heaven and will make war with the saints.

Abaddon and his army will be given victory over the army of heaven. This event will surely bring fear to the hearts of every child of God. Doubt will reign as the fear overtakes mankind and they experience the **victory** of evil.

But then we read in Daniel 8:16 *"And I heard a man's voice....saying "Gabriel, make this man understand the vision........the vision refers to the time of the end....when the transgressors have reached their fullness and their power is mighty..... He shall rise against the Prince of princes; but he shall be broken without human means".* (NKLV)

Revelation 17:14 reassures us: *"These will make war with the Lamb, and the Lamb will overcome them, for He isLord of lords and King of kings; and those who are with Him are called, chosen, and faithful."*

Ephesians 3: 3, 4, 8, 9 tells us: *"How by revelation he made known unto me; (...Whereby.* **When ye read, ye may understand my knowledge** *in the mystery of Christ.) Which* **in other ages was not made known** *unto the sons of men, as it is now revealed unto his holy apostles and prophets by the*

*Spirit.....unto me, who am less than the least of all saints, is this grace given, that I should preach among the Gentiles the unsearchable riches of Christ; And to make all men see what is the fellowship of the mystery, which from the beginning of the world **hath been hid** in God who created all things...."*

These verses tell us that there is a mystery to the Bible and that this mystery is opened only to those who seek its answers with a pure heart. Interestingly, they also tell us that to many, these mysteries will remain hidden, remain a secret kept from those who do not desire to learn of God.

Thus, we will keep searching scripture, keep asking God to open our hearts to His word and message, and help us help others as well as ourselves.

"As For Me

And My House,

We Shall Serve

The Lord",

Joshua 24:15

Chapter Four

GOD'S PLAN OF SALVATION

It is amazing to see the plans God made for His creation. And to see the incredible all encompassing manner in which God cares for those who will live with Him for all eternity in a sin-free Universe. What we learn is that God, knowing man would sin, desired that mankind have a way out from under the captivity Satan would have over them.

Thus God arranged for man to learn of good and evil so he would have the opportunity to freely choose good, to repent of all evil, and to seek the forgiveness of his sin. This would mean that man could freely choose to have a life with God and not with Satan. Thus God gave mankind everything he needed to break free of Satan and allow God and His statutes to fill their heart and ransom them from Satan's captivity.

Scripture teaches us that God longs to fill His new kingdom with souls who will truly love one another, and love His Son and Him above all things. Matthew 22:37-39 says, "*Jesus said unto him, Thou shalt love the Lord thy God with all thy heart, and with all thy soul, and with all thy mind. This is the first and great commandment. And the second is like unto it, Thou shalt love thy neighbor as thyself.*" God wants these souls to understand the value of love, trust, and loyalty, and to practice these attributes voluntarily. (John 14:23)

God began His plan by creating the earth in its limited universe. Then He created Adam and Eve to live happily in the Garden of Eden, walking and talking with Him. But the angel Lucifer, later known as Satan, rebelled against God because he was jealous of Christ, and of the new being, man, who God planned to elevate above the angels. (Isaiah 14:12-15) As a result of his rebellion, Satan was thrown to earth with the angels (Revelation 12:9) who followed Satan and thereby had also disobeyed God. These numbered one-third of all the angels. These are known today as the "fallen angels" and sometimes referred to as "demonic".

No one knows exactly how many angels God created but we do know that no new angels have been made since God first created them. In terms of how many angels exist, scripture tells us in Revelations 5:11: *"Then I looked and heard the voice of many angels, **numbering thousands upon thousands, and ten thousand times ten thousand.***

They encircled the throne and the living creatures and the elders."

Satan knew God's plan and understood that when God's plan was completed, and God had obtained the number of faithful loving souls He longed for, Satan would be thrown into Hell for what he had done and with him *all* evil would be forever bound. The fallen angels would also be confined to the Lake of Fire with Satan where they can no longer harm or tempt the children of God. Thus, to prevent God's plan from moving forward and forestall his own destruction, Satan destroyed God's relationship of trust and loyalty with Adam and Eve by enticing them to sin through disobedience. Satan knew that sin would automatically separate man from God because of God's perfect righteousness. Therefore, God had to banish Adam and Eve as he had banished Satan. (Genesis 3:1 and Genesis 3:23)

But God, knowing what Satan would do, provided a way for Adam and Eve, and the generations to follow, to escape the captivity of Satan through the forgiveness of sin. In fact, this is why Christ offered Himself as the perfect sacrifice by which the sins of man could be forgiven. (John 1:29) At every turn, Satan interfered with God's plan, working to destroy those who tried to follow God. He knew that when God collected the number of souls He desired for His new creation, Satan would be bound forever. Thus Satan is fighting for his life when trying to draw us into sin.

However, because of God's love, many of those tested by Satan are strengthened through his attacks, becoming like gold refined in the fires of tribulation. From these faithful, God is building what the Bible calls *The Bride of Christ*. God also provided for those who died in sin both before and after Christ provided His sacrifice by creating a means of testimony in eternity. Thus while grace is still available on earth, it is also available in eternity. Christ entered hell after His death to provide testimony of His triumph to those who had died in their sins before He could bring His perfect sacrifice. (Luke 24:46) He told these souls that now they too could find forgiveness. (1Timothy 2:4) However, both grace on earth *and* in eternity will last only for a specific amount of time which God has planned for the Bride to be "made ready" for the day of the First Resurrection. (Acts 1:6-7)

When that time is up, God will send His Son back to earth for the First Resurrection (Revelation 20:5) when He will take to heaven both those from eternity who have obtained forgiveness and those alive who have remained faithful. (2Peter 3:10) When they are gone, grace will also be gone, and the final destruction of the end times will begin on the earth where, among other things, one-third of all the people on earth will die. When the destruction ends, God will send His Son back to earth with those He had taken at the First Resurrection. These souls will have celestial (perfect) bodies, and will reign as kings and priests for one thousand years of peace to bring testimony to everyone living or dead who was not taken in the First Resurrection.

Satan will be bound during this time, unable to influence mankind, so all of mankind will learn about and accept God. But, after the one thousand years of peace, Satan will be loosed again for a little while so those who have now newly accepted God can be tested. (Revelation 20:7) Satan will wreak havoc on those not firm in their faith and many will leave God and follow him. (Revelation 20:2) Then the Day of Judgment will arrive when *everyone* who was ever born, or conceived, except those taken by Christ for the First Resurrection, *will be judged.*

Some of these people, who the Bible calls the *"goats"*, will be cast into hell with Satan forever, while others, called the *"lambs"*, will inhabit God's new kingdom where there will be no sorrow and no tears. The goats, and Satan and his angels, will be cast into the lake of fire and brimstone and because the soul never dies, will be ***tormented day and***

night forever. (Revelation 20:10 and 15)   Those who are taken for the First Resurrection will continue to reign as kings and priests in the new kingdom and live in the City of God.   They will never have to be judged because their sins were forgiven, and entirely wiped away by God.

Also important for us to know is that God longs for a **specific number of souls** to be a part of the Bride of Christ.   This is mentioned in scripture and also mentioned in the Apocrypha.   11 Esdras 2:40-41 says, *"Receive they number O Sion, and embrace those of thine that are clothed in white which have fulfilled the law of the Lord.* **The number of thy children whom thou longest for, is fulfilled:** *beseech the Lord that thy people, which have been called from the beginning, may be hallowed."*

Our desire as Christians is to work toward the completion of God's work here on earth, labor in faith, love, and longsuffering to make ourselves worthy to be a child of God and become a part of the Bide of Christ. To accomplish this goal we learn God's words, put on the armor of God, seek forgiveness, strive to be an overcomer, and wait patiently for the completion of God's Plan of Salvation, and the return of His Son. We carry the hope in our hearts that soon God will find the last soul. Romans 8:25 tells us, *"But if we hope for that we see not, then do we with patience wait for it."*

But there is also a far more sinister part to the story of salvation. It is the time when evil gains the victory over God. It is when God's children will be subjected to every evil ever known to man and plead for death because it will be such a difficult time in which to live. Thus God warns us to **prepare**, to **know** *His words,* **understand** *the horrors* yet to come, **learn** how putting on the armour of God can help. More importantly, believe that victory **_will_** be God's and we must remain strong until then.

The Bible is a wonderful resource for us and it speaks often of the *glory* of God and of the *wonder* of faith and prayer and of the *beauty* of the coming world of which we can be a part. But it is also a book which relates the horrors of a battle between good and evil which is so fierce that mankind can barely deal with it. This battle is often referred to as "Spiritual Warfare" and has been ongoing since Man was placed into the Garden of Eden.

The battle between good and evil teaches us about an evil so venomous and so deadly and so powerful that we will be in shock seeing what will occur. We may not understand why God does not intervene, why He seems impotent. But this is why God is warning us *now* about fear; about an assault on our faith. He knows what is to come and wants to warn us; wants us to arm ourselves with every godly weapon available so we do not lose our faith, so we CAN stand strong when every fiber of our body feels defeated.

We may not recognize the depth of suffering yet to come because we are spoiled. We have enjoyed God's blessings; we have lived in a country which allows us to freely worship; we have not seen the real face of evil....yet. While we know of evil, read of evil, see evil via the television, we have been relatively protected and do not yet realize what evil will bring us in the future. God is afraid for us. He clearly speaks to us about fear, about losing our faith, about putting on the armour of God to survive those days of evil. We however are like children who see no need for a raincoat just because it's raining. We are fearless because we have not known real fear. But God is warning us. God is knocking on our hearts door to get our attention. God wants us to heed His words and prepare.

God comforts us with the words from Proverbs3:10-12, which says *"....then your barns will be filled to overflowing and your vats will brim over with new wine. My child, don't reject the Lord.....don't be upset when he corrects you...."*

And in Revelation 21:4 we are told: *"And God will wipe away all tears from their eyes. There will be no more death, or mourning or crying or pain, for the old order of things has passed away."*

And In Revelation 20:14: *"....and death and hell were cast into the Lake of Fire....."*

In Psalm 91:15-16 God promises: *"He shall call upon me, and I will answer him. I will be with him in trouble; I will deliver him, and honour him."*

God wants us to trust Him and tells us that if we continue on in faith, the end reward will be worth the struggle. 1 Corinthians 15:58 says: *"Therefore my beloved brethren, be ye stedfast, unmovable, always abounding in the work of the Lord, forasmuch as ye know that your labour is not in vain of the Lord."*

Chapter Five

ANGELS, GIANTS & THE BIBLE

When we think of angels, we think of the chubby adorable children with wings and arrows who speak of love on Valentine's Day. Or we think of a beautiful winged adult in flowing white robes who brings us a special message or provides us with protection. We never think of sin or of evil when we think of angels. We forget that one third of ALL angels rebelled against God and began an era of evil against mankind. We forget that scripture addresses these fallen angels as demonic! Seldom do we associate Satan and his wrath as a constant war against not only God, but also against the children of God. Nor do we think of a cunning, malignant being whose primary goal is to destroy the faith of God's children and block the completion of God's Plan of Salvation.

Revelation 12:7-9 tells us: *"Now war arose in heaven, Michael and his angels fighting against the dragon. And the dragon and his angels fought back, but he was defeated, and there was no longer any place for them in heaven. And the great dragon was thrown down, that ancient serpent, who is called the devil and Satan, the deceiver of the whole world— he was thrown down to the earth, and his angels were thrown down with him."*

1 John: 4:1 warns: *"Beloved, do not believe every spirit, but test the spirits to see whether they are from God, for many false prophets have gone out into the world."* This tells us that we can be easily

deceived by entities which are not godly and that we must protect our spiritual life carefully. The fallen angels who followed Satan tried to harm and influence mankind by causing them to sin thereby blocking their relationship with God.

There were also fallen angels who influenced some of the women living on earth and mated with them. The children born from the union between a fallen angel and a child of God were called the Nephilim and were giants. They were so large that the Bible refers to ordinary men as looking like "grasshoppers" in comparison. They were evil to the core and caused sin to escalate at an alarming pace. They and their children passed on their sinful nature to each generation. All Nephilim were great sinners and were also perverted in their way of life. In fact, scripture speaks of Sodom and Gomorrah and its sin in connection with the Nephilim giants. In the process of having children, the fallen angels the Nephilim passed along their sinful nature through their genes.

There are many scriptural references to these giants in Genesis 6:4, Numbers 13:31, 33, Deuteronomy 2:10-11, 21 and 3:11, Ezekiel 28, Job 2:1, Jude 1:6,-8, Peter 2:4, Colossian 2:15, Peter 2:4, Genesis 3:15 and 6:5 to name a few. Genesis 6:4 tells us: *"There were giants in the earth in those days and also after that when the sons of god came in unto the daughters of men, and they bore children to them. The same became mighty men which were of old, men of renown. And God saw that the wickedness of man was great in the earth, and that every imagination of the thoughts of his heart was only evil. And it repented the Lord that He had made man on the earth and it grieved Him at His heart. And the Lord said, I will destroy man whom I created from the face of the earth; both man and beast, and the creeping thing and the fowl of the air, for it repenteth me that I have made them."*

As God saw yet another arena through which "inherited sin" could escalate among mankind, He became angry and decided to send the flood to destroy this dangerous line. God saved only Noah and his family to protect the lineage He was establishing for the advent of Christ. Thus God warned Noah to ready himself for the deluge, the flood which destroyed all men except those in Noah's family. Noah and his family spurned sin and loved God and because of his faith, Noah and his family were spared. 2 Peter 2:4 tells us the fate of these angels saying *"For if God spared not the angels that sinned, but cast them down to hell, and delivered them into chains of darkness to be reserved unto judgment; and spared not the old world, but saved Noah the eighth person, a preacher of righteousness, bringing in the flood upon the world of the ungodly."*

Amazingly however, God's incredible love, longsuffering and forbearance even toward the fallen angels who sinned so incessantly and rebelled so vehemently against God were given consideration in the eternity where they languished in the prison of hell.

2 Peter 3:19 tells us that Christ, when He died on the cross for our sins, went into the realms where sinners languished (even to these angels) to bring them testimony. *"By which he also went and preached unto the spirits in prison: which sometimes were disobedient, when once the longsuffering God waited in the days of Noah, while the ark was a preparing, wherein few, that is eight souls were saved by water."*

Scripture explains that Satan's plan was to ruin the lineage of the coming Messiah and assisting in inspiring all mankind to become increasingly evil. While evil itself remained, it was slowed as the flood secured the lineage of Christ through Noah and destroyed the fallen angel's lineage. Even so, God was exceedingly sorrowful that he'd become so angry that he'd had to bring the flood to harm mankind.

Could this be one of the reasons why God will allow Satan his freedom "for a little while" when the Thousand Year reign of peace ends? Will this time period produce the fear of which God warns and break our faith? Could this be the final test of those who were not taken at the First Resurrection? Could this be why God speaks about fear throughout scripture? Revelation 2:10 tells us *"Fear none of these things which thou shalt suffer: behold the devil shall cast some of you into prison, that ye may be tried, and ye shall have tribulation ten days: be thou faithful unto death, and I will give thee a crown of life."*

At the same time God encourages us to love Him fully with an open heart and not with a half measure. Revelation 3:15 warns: *"I know thy works, you are neither cold nor hot: I would thou wert cold or hot. So then because thou art lukewarm, and neither cold nor hot, I will spue thee out of my mouth."* Revelation 6:9 tells us: *"And when he had opened the fifth seal, I saw under the altar the souls of them that were slain for the word of God and for the testimony which they held."*

Many of these verses do stir a great fear in our heart because they seem to warn that children of God will not only suffer a great deal, but then finally be killed for *believing* in God. Could this be the result of removing all vestiges of our faith from schools and government? Could this warning be about what may be just around the corner for all Christians?

However, we are comforted by the words in Revelation 7:16 which tell us: *"They shall hunger no more, neither thirst anymore, neither shall the sun light on them, nor any heat. For the Lamb which is in the midst of the throne shall feed them, and shall lead them unto living fountains of waters: and God shall wipe away all tears from their eyes."* We must remember that there ARE **good** angels. In fact two thirds of all the angels ever created have remained faithful to God and are beneficial to God's Plan of Salvation. Angels, Archangels and Principalities are the angels who appear to mankind and step in to protect them when needed. These angels reside in the realm of Heaven which is closest to earth. They are aware of what is occurring on earth and act as messengers of God by inspiring men in their daily lives. Some of these angels inspired the hearts and minds of those who wrote scripture. These angels can perform acts on earth which re-direct a potentially lethal situation to help someone in distress. Scripture tells us that a time to die is pre-appointed by God thus sometimes these angels intervene to cement the time of such a destiny.

Both Biblical scripture and the Apocryphal books of scripture describe the work of Gabriel, Michael, Raphael and Uriel who are four of the purported seven archangels who surround the throne of God. Scripture describes Michael's activities as those of a warrior fighting to help us and also fighting for God against Satan. The apostle John recorded a vision he had which mentions Michael: *"War broke out in heaven: Michael and his angels fought with the dragon; and the dragon and his angels fought"* (Revelation 12:7). This reveals what we would think of as opposing captains or generals commanding their respective armies. Michael, a holy, righteous angel, is depicted in scripture as leading the righteous angels in a fight against the "dragon" which is Satan, the chief of the demons, and against the spirit beings (fallen angels) following Satan. (See also Matthew 25:31, 41; Revelation 20:2). Scripture describes Gabriel's activities as those of a protector as when he closed the mouth of the lions when Daniel was thrown into the Lion's den.(Daniel 8:16, Daniel 9:2, Luke 1:19) Gabriel was also the messenger who told Zachariah of the pending birth of John the Baptist and told Mary that she would bear the Son of God.

Few are familiar with the Apocrypha which can be found in many Bibles between the Old and the New Testaments. The Apocrypha consists of 14 "books" which were originally attached to the Greek Old Testament, but not in the Hebrew-written Bible because they were "first-written" in the Greek language. However to the Jews the Apocrophal books were considered scripture and used by the Jews at the time of Christ. About 60 years after the crucifixion of Christ, a group of Rabbi's canonized a

Hebrew scripture. Any work of scripture not originally written in Hebrew was discarded. However, the early Christians retained the Greek Old Testament, because the pagan world spoke Greek and would be brought testimony in this language.

When Christ's disciples wrote the New Testament books, they, too were composed in the same Greek language, allowing the world at large to read them and is why, in prophecy, Jesus, quoting Isaiah, announced that He would speak to the Jewish people in a *foreign* language which was the Greek just mentioned. The early Christian Church in the first century A.D. quickly coalesced into two Roman churches, one in the east, which we call today Eastern Orthodox, and the other in the west now called Roman Catholic. Both adopted the Greek Old Testament.

Consequently early Catholic scholars assigned the questionable Greek-written books of the Apocrypha to a middle category, coining the term "Apocrypha" which meant "hidden" to define them. The title was not meant to disparage their claim to divine inspiration, but to suggest that their content was more for scholars because of the hidden nature of the revelations they contained. These scholars felt that the general public was not sufficiently enlightened to readily understand them. Orthodox and Roman Catholic churches represent about 75% of the world's Christians, so acceptance of these books as true scripture is substantial in the modern Christian community.

Many years later, the King James Version of the Bible (also known as the Authorized Version) was translated. This was completed in 1611 and is termed a "version" rather than a translation because it was not translated from the original languages (Hebrew and Greek). Instead, it was translated from the various other translations. Where there was discrepancy or inconsistency, the translators went back to the original languages to determine what the correct translation should be. This version contained the Apocrypha. At a later date, another committee was formed which determined that the books of the Apocrypha were not works which had been "inspired" by God and the apocrypha was removed from future revisions of the King James Version of the Holy Bible. I find however that much of the information in the Apocrypha, especially what we read in Esdras, is not only closely related to what the Bible tells us, but adds much more information to the verses we find in the "approved" version of scripture.

What we cannot find in regular scripture can often be found in the Apocrypha. For instance, the Archangel Raphael first appears in the apocryphal Book of Tobit (12:15) and also in the apocryphal Book of Enoch. Here we find that he is known for his abilities to heal and also for being the angel who tells Noah how to prepare for the flood. Also in the Apocrypha, in 2 Esdras, we find the archangel Uriel who God sends to answer a series of questions the prophet Ezra asks of God. When answering Ezra's questions, Uriel tells him that God has permitted him to describe signs about good and evil at work in the world, but it will still be difficult for Ezra to understand from his limited human perspective. In 2 Esdras 4:10-11, Uriel states: *"You cannot understand the things with which you have grown up; how then can your mind comprehend the way of the Most High? And how can one who is already worn out by the corrupt world understand incorruption?"* When Ezra asks questions about his personal life, such as how long he'll live, Uriel replies: *"Concerning the signs about which you ask me, I can tell you in part; but I was not sent to tell you concerning your life, for I do not know."*(2 Esdras 4:52) Each of these archangels fought for God's will to be done despite Satan's attempt to thwart God's plan.

Psalm 91:11 tells us that we can call upon the angels for help because God ordained that they listen to men and help them where they can. *"For he shall give his angels charge over thee, to keep thee in all thy ways."*

Reading 11 Esdras Chapter Four in the Apocrypha beautifully relates a conversation Esdra is allowed to have with God. In verse 22 of Chapter four, Esdras asks God: *"....I beseech thee, O Lord, let me have an understanding:......"* And in verse 26 God replies to Esdras saying: *"The more thou searchest, the more thou shalt be astonished....."* Then in verse 27 says:*"....And cannot comprehend what is promised to the righteous in the future time....."*. In verse 28 God says: *"...the evil is sown, but the destruction thereof is not yet come."*

Interestingly in Verse 37 in answer to Esdras' question about when God's plan will be completed, Esdras is told: *"For God has weighed the time upon a scale, and measured the years with a measure, and diligently counted the days, and will change nothing until the previously designated measure is fulfilled."*

HELEN GLOWACKI

Chapter Six

THRONES AND CHARIOTS

Sadly, so many good people are complacent about the importance of God's Plan of Salvation. They appear to be oblivious to the fact that the children of God are destined to engage in a great battle where those who fight them will have immense power and will initially overcome them. This alone is enough to bring fear to our hearts and to cause us to wonder when all this will happen and whether we can even survive the fear this can cause. Scripture tells us that this will be a time when those who did not listen to God will gnash their teeth in terror and waste away. (Psalm 112:10)

It is not that man is always afraid to die, but many are afraid of the "process" of dying which can easily make us fearful of death itself. Many of us have seen our loved ones die and realize that the process is not always an easy one. Scripture describes life *after* death as "torment" for those who have not sought God, while those who did know God are described as "resting in the arms of Abraham". This tells us that the state of being dead itself is not something to be feared unless we have never sought God nor sought forgiveness.

As the prospect of death approaches we must realize that what the world sees as success or failure is not true success or failure in God's eyes. This is evidenced by an interesting parable which Christ brought to us.

In the parable of the Rich man and Lazarus for example, found in Luke 16:19-31, the rich man, when he dies finds himself in torment. But Lazarus, the beggar, who ate only crumbs at the end of the walk leading to the rich man's house, and who the world viewed as a failure, is described in scripture as being transported from the state of death to a place where Abraham could comfort him.

The rich man was astounded by where he found himself once he died and admits to being in torture. He begs for God to send Lazarus to his brothers so they do not end up as he has. But God tells him he is too late, that his brothers, like him, would simply not listen. Their hearts, like the Rich man's, had hardened toward God and His statutes.

Sadly, few of us acknowledge the repercussions of the life we lead and the decisions we make as affecting the eternal life of our soul. Our arrogance is so immense that we often simply believe that we are okay as we are. Many do not consider that *there are only three places* the soul (which never dies) can occupy once God's Plan of Salvation is complete. These are The City of God, The Kingdom of God, or The Lake of Fire. And few accept that that there *are* pre-requisites (rules) for entering each of these places.

The City of God has been created for the Bride of Christ who are those who remain faithful and those who Christ will take at the First Resurrection. *These souls will be a part of the household of God.* They will live for all eternity in the gated City where God the Father, Christ our Lord, and the Holy Spirit will dwell. They will hold positions of esteem.

The Kingdom of God has been created for the Lambs of God who will be redeemed on Judgment Day. They will live *outside* the city gates in the

Kingdom of God where there will never again be sorrow or tears. They will have access to God and the Lord Jesus and live under the theocracy which will be governed with love.

The Lake of Fire has been created for Satan and his demonic angels, and for those which scripture calls "the goats". The Lake of Fire will confine evil thus separate good from evil for all eternity. The "goats" are those who will be judged and found lacking on Judgment Day. They did not seek God, and did not desire to meet the requirements necessary to enter God's kingdom which *the rules of God's righteousness demanded.*

The New Kingdom which God will create for those who love Him is the culmination of God's Plan of Salvation where evil will be *forever* separated from good. This kingdom is exclusively created for those who love God and who made the effort to express that love by learning and striving to obey God's words. As we await the return of Christ and strive to become the Bride of Christ who will be taken at the First Resurrection, God asks us to teach others about Christ and instruct others how they can obtain grace and forgiveness.

Scripture teaches that when Christ died for our sins He made grace available to **everyone**. This offer was for those still living on earth and also to every soul in eternity who died in sin. Since we are all sinners, and each of us have been taught the many aspects of sin, we are asked to develop and extend compassion to those who remain active in those sins and to those who died in those sins. We are not to condone these sins, but to teach how grace can erase them from a truly remorseful heart. This is why our testimony remains an important task for all of God's children…..as does their behavior for being a role model to others.

God asks us to intercede for the souls in eternity who have **remorse**, who **acknowledge**their sins, who truly **repent**, and who **forgive** others. He asks us to reach out to these lost souls through our understanding, our compassion and our prayers. He teaches that we must never pray _to_ these souls in eternity but to our Heavenly Father, asking that they be drawn to the altar of grace while grace is still available. Having died in sin, the souls trapped in their sins in eternity live in bleak conditions where fear and chaos reign. Though they hear our prayers, and thus know that we too have lived through some of what they have lived through, they often cannot find the courage to respond. They have little trust in their hearts. Thus we must continue in our efforts to draw these souls to God through our love, compassion and intercession. God is pleased when our prayers expand over time to include *all* types of sinners because it is an indication that we have overcome our personal feelings of anger and hate and judgment.

As we prepare our hearts to accept these souls as they are, pray for them daily, and harbour no grudge for what they did, they begin to trust again and consider coming to the altar of grace to see what is offered. Many may come and sit under the Word and still not respond. Some may never respond and will become a part of the goats who will be cast into the Lake of Fire. But some will come, some will desire to repent for and overcome their failures.

Those who do not accept will suffer what scripture \calls ***the second death*** when they are thrown into the Lake of Fire. ***The second death is forever. It is inescapable and it is a torture for all eternity since the soul never dies.*** But all of us have our free will. God does not want us forcibly dragged into His presence but to come, gladly, willingly with an open heart. God provides everyone with an opportunity to come to Him using many venues to draw them. Many accept but sadly many are too complacent, too comfortable with where they are that they will not heed the invitation and will remain where they are. It is amazing to consider how God could possibly know all that He does and also look into our hearts to learn what really motivates us.

Scripture, as we have already discussed, tells us that the angels who serve God also act as messengers for Him and to Him. They are given instruction and can intervene in our lives. Thus they can also answer prayers which have reached God's ears and received God's blessing.

In the tenets of Judaism and Christianity, guardian angels carry out God's will when answering prayers. Angels may also help people plead their cases before God to try to influence His will and how it's carried out. Genesis chapter 32 of the Torah and Holy Bible record how the prophet Jacob wrestled with an angel overnight to try to convince God to give him a blessing, and the angel finally tells him that God has decided to give Jacob the blessing he was seeking. Verses 26 through 28 describe how the struggle ends: *"Then the man [angel] said, 'Let me go, for it is daybreak.' But Jacob replied, 'I will not let you go unless you bless me.' The man asked him, 'What is your name?'. 'Jacob,' he answered. Then the man said, 'Your name will no longer be Jacob, but Israel, because you have struggled with God and with humans and have overcome.'*

The answer to our prayers is an incredible gift which demonstrates God's power and also His concern for us. Therefore, we must pray diligently for ourselves and for others. God rewards this effort as it is a sign that we are aware of our sinful nature and that we care for others, and are willing to extend ourselves to others. God sees all and knows all and according to scripture utilizes a great chariot which moves at immense speed and in any direction. Scripture addresses the make-up of this vehicle by describing the wheels which carry the chariot and explains that these "wheels" are angels with a multitude of eyes which watch those on earth.

Ezekiel 1:5-28 describes a vision Ezekiel had about angels who are called the "Thrones". They are also mentioned as the "Wheels" and are one of the higher ranking angels in God's army. The Thrones both guard and move God's chariot. Ezekiel tells us that these angels have many eyes which are attached to the entire circle of the two wheels. We are also told that the chariots have the ability to move up and down and side to side and to turn. Their appearance is that of a wheel within a wheel, and the ring of each of the wheels are, according to Ezekiel, full of eyes to scan the earth and watch where they are going. When they stood still, they let down their wings and shone like a sapphire. When they moved they became amber colored with the brightness of fire surrounding them.

Ezekiel's vision of the four wheels illustrates the omnipresence and omniscience of God and is associated with the "four living creatures" (Ezekiel 1:4), later described as cherubim (Ezekiel 10:5, 20), who are angelic beings appointed as guardians of the   Holiness   of   God.

Each wheel is described as two parts in one, with one inside the other at right angles which enables these angels to move God's chariot in any direction instantly without having to turn. They move like a flash of lightning and have the appearance of a topaz or other semiprecious stone. The outer rim of the wheels is described as high and awesome with the outer edge of the rims inset with "eyes". (Ezekiel 1:14-18)

The Spirit or life of these angels or living creatures as they were sometimes described is in the wheels (Ezekiel 1:20-21) which allows them to move as desired. Ezekiel tells us that these creatures obtain information about the direction they are to go from the Spirit of God through direct knowledge of and access to God's will. Their mobility is to suggest the omnipresence of God; the eyes to suggest God's omniscience; and the elevated position, His omnipotence. This vision appeared to Ezekiel as a powerful image of movement and action characteristic of God's divine nature and presented God on a chariot-like throne. The image also projected God's glory and the extension of that glory into the universe. The vision of the cherubim, the chariot, the Spirit, the wheels and the action emphasized a great unity or bond between God and the   Cherubim.

One of the angels God created are described as being living "creatures" whose name means "ones of love". They have six wings, and four faces; one an ox, one a lion, one an eagle and one, a man. While a terrifying vision, the vision displays the majesty and glory of God and represents God's creativity, power and glory. (Ezekiel 1:28) Nevertheless, unless mankind is taught that these "creatures" are angels they would be terribly frightened to encounter them.

The lesson for us today is that, through His marvelous providence, God moves in the affairs of all nations to work out His own perfect but unseen plan. He is always at work, His plan is intricately designed, never wrong, and never late. (Romans 8:28).

Many scholars now liken the vision Ezekiel presents in scripture as being similar to eye witness accounts and photos of UFO's and a foretelling of how God will *"....come in fire and His chariots, like the whirlwind, to render His anger with fury and His rebuke with flames of fire."* (Isaiah 66:15)

2 Kings 2:11 recounts the time when Elijah was taken to heaven in a fiery chariot: *"Then it happened, as they continued on and talked, that suddenly a chariot of fire appeared with horses of fire, and separated the two of them; and Elijah went up by a whirlwind into heaven".* Psalm 68:17 tells us, *"The chariots of God are twenty thousand, even thousands of angels."* And Ezekiel 10:5, 20 tells us that *"The wheels of God's chariots are Cherubim."*

It does seem that the description of the movements and vision of God's chariots as outlined in scripture could fit the description of and movements of what we know about UFO's. Perhaps if such information becomes more wide spread and provable, this too could shake our faith and create fear in our hearts for it is a new way to look at God and what power He wields.

Perhaps all these questions are foolish questions; perhaps they are not based in fact and can cause undue concern. But it is better to be prepared for all potential possibilities rather than for none. It is better to keep in mind God's immense power and total control of the Universe and not denigrate Him to fitting into a mold which we, in our limited capacity, have created for Him.

It is also important to understand that God created diversity in the angel world and each is beautiful in His eyes even though if we did not know what we were witnessing, we might become fearful. Thus just the simple description of the appearance of some of God's angels may be enough to allay our fears should we encounter them.

Our job is to arm ourselves with as much knowledge about scripture as we can. Our job is to prepare ourselves for whatever new knowledge will be added to our lives. Our job is to welcome our Heavenly Father being all powerful and in total control of the universe, and offering so much more than we could imagine. Our job is to.....above all.... continue to trust God with our present and our future. Our job is to learn what knowledge God wants us to gain so we are ready for any onslaught to our faith! Our job is to learn what we need so we can be found worthy to be a part of God's kingdom.

God tells us in Revelation 22:7 *"Behold, I am coming quickly! Blessed is he who keeps the words of the prophecy of this book."*

Chapter Seven

LACK OF KNOWLEDGE

As we look back at the information we have covered in the previous chapters, we can see that there has indeed been much we did not know and much that we can still learn. We can see from the verses which tell us that evolution is after all compatible with Creation that we can read scripture and not fully understand what it is telling us until

God opens our understanding. This supports God's words about the Bible being a mystery not unveiled to everyone especially not to those who wish to use the Bible to **_disprove_** God's promises. Even if all the verses in scripture which we have discussed are familiar to us, perhaps the discussion of how to apply that knowledge makes us look at all things related to our faith a bit differently. Perhaps it helps us realize that there may be much more in scripture yet to be unveiled and that we might read a verse today and then tomorrow recognize such a greater meaning than we'd previously seen.

Our learning process will never end while we are here on earth. We may find ourselves sitting at the feet of Jesus tomorrow and still have a myriad of questions for Him. However, many say that we will be so happy to find ourselves with Christ that we will no longer need the answers to any of our questions. Sadly, there will also be those who will find themselves locked out of God's presence and hear Him say *"I know ye not"* as scripture warns.

We are a curious people. Many desire to learn and can acknowledge that our Universe contains so many mysteries about how it works that we may never have all our questions answered. Many count on our faith to carry us through, and count on our commitment to our Heavenly Father to keep us faithful despite information which could be difficult to accept.

Most of us are deeply convinced that the path we have chosen is the right path for us. We believe that we have chosen our path with our own free will and must sometimes dig deeply into our hearts to pull up the trust in God we need to keep us on that path...or for some....to put us *on* that path. But what about those who remain as they are and do not actively engage with God? Can we be sure that God will call them? How can we help them heed such a call?

A few months ago I wrote an article to post on Face Book which addressed the plight of a young girl trapped in a cold dark valley who prayed that God would help her leave that valley, climb the mountain and be free.

Here is a small excerpt from that article:

"Once upon a time a child of God found herself transported to the darkest valley imaginable. The valley was surrounded by a tall mountain range. She hadn't expected to find herself in such a place and as she looked around, she was chilled by the lack of warmth and sunlight. Her circumstances brought fear to her heart.

Over time, knowing that the valley was not where she wanted to be, she wondered why she stayed in the valley where she was so unhappy and began to look more carefully for an avenue of escape. She could see the many majestic mountain peaks surrounding the valley, but also saw one path on each of the mountains which appeared to reach the very top.

She wondered if she could walk toward one of those paths, find it, and begin the climb to leave the valley. She knew that she would have to choose which path she would take, but not knowing what she would face on such a journey, she was afraid. So she prayed and asked God to show her the path which would be right for her, the one He wanted her to take.

God heard the prayers of His child and He answered them. He summoned the sun to shine behind one of the mountain peaks and send its light over the clouds and the blue backdrop of the skies. He summoned the birds to fly over the path He chose for her to demonstrate that if the birds could reach the majestic peaks, so could she.

As she began to recognize the signs God was sending to her, she decided to walk across the valley and find the pathway filled with sunlight and chirping birds. As she began her trek, a storm suddenly appeared in front of her. The path ahead filled with lightning and with torrential rains. She watched as the side of the path became muddy and the small plants alongside slid away. She watched as trees split from the lightning, she was afraid to move forward. So, she turned back.

Sadly, she stayed in the valley once again; in the cold and the dark, and she cried. She wondered if she would ever be free to walk again in the sunlight. She wondered if she would ever know where God wanted her to be. She wondered what it was that she was to learn from this terrible experience. She longed to find the courage to leave.

She continued to pray. Finally, she asked God why He'd pointed her toward a path and then made it almost impossible to pass. She asked God to help her understand and to show her what she was to do. She prayed that she could open her heart to what God wanted for her and quell her fear.

*She began to listen to the little voice inside her, knowing that it was the Holy Spirit of God reaching out to speak with her. She heard the voice ask: "Do you trust God....really trust Him?" She pondered this question carefully. She suddenly realized that she had fully believed that she **did** trust God, but by being afraid to take the path she had been shown, she had not **really** been willing to trust after all.*

*She was surprised by this thought because she'd felt quite strongly that she **had** trusted God. So she prayed again and asked for forgiveness and asked God to give her another chance. The same voice responded and asked: "What if the lightning never struck the area where you would have walked? What if the mudslides never actually touched the path? What if the trees which split fell only to the side of the path?"*

And she was ashamed by those questions. She saw that God had simply wanted her to trust Him and she had not done so. She realized that God wanted to bring her onto a path which would bring her into the sunshine again. He wanted to show her how much He loved her and cared for her. But she had to have trust in God to achieve that goal.

God's child prayed yet again and asked God to give her courage, to fill her with strength and perseverance, and to bind the evil forces which brought fear to her heart. And God answered her prayer and did help her overcome her fear. And so God's child finally found the path God had set before her and with trust and courage, she began her climb.

This time she reached the top of the mountain and saw before her the light of the sun, the blue of the skies and the soft, puffy white clouds. She saw flowers, and trees and happy little villages. She thanked God for His help and promised to trust Him and follow His statutes all the days of her life.

The moral of this story is that we often hold *ourselves* back from receiving the fullness of God's blessings. It is usually our complacency which holds us back but can also be our fear of change. Fear and mistrust disconnects us from the loving protection God always offers us. Once we make the decision to grasp God's hand and allow Him to guide us, we will never walk through any valley alone. We will instead come out of our trials and tribulations safe and protected and changed for the better!

That little story should help us realize that what causes our immobility is our *inactivity* it is our lack of faith which holds us back from recognizing the importance of actively seeking and knowing God which prevents change.

God emphatically tells us he fears that those He loves could be lost through their lack of understanding. This statement is very powerful. We believe that God can do anything thus could easily help us learn enough not to fail. But many do not accept that it is their own responsibility to seek God. Why? What have we missed? Are we that weak? Are we that lazy? Or is Satan that strong?

Hosea 4:1 tells us: *"Hear the word of the Lord, ye children of Israel: for **the Lord hath a controversy** with the inhabitants of the land, **because there is no truth, nor mercy, nor knowledge of God** in the land."*

Hosea 4:6 warns: *"**My people are destroyed for lack of knowledge: because thou hast rejected knowledge, I will also reject thee, that thou shalt be no priest to me: seeing thou hast forgotten the law of thy God, I will also forget thy children**".*

These words are addressed to those who take no interest in learning God's words or exercising His admonitions. They are addressed to those who believe they are "good" people already and have no need to study the word of God. They justify this decision by stating that they "love" God and know "enough" about God to be accepted into His new kingdom. While these people accept that without a passport they cannot enter another country they refuse to believe there may be rules about entering God's new kingdom!

Is the commitment we must make too difficult to achieve? Do we simply have such a lack of knowledge that we do not realize what is required of us? Are we so arrogant that we do not acknowledge that God's plan will move forward without us?

There is an interesting example of those who do not know scripture, yet claim to "know enough" and thereby make a huge spiritual mistake. These are those who emphatically state that Jesus Christ was married to Mary Magdalene. This is false doctrine placed into the heart by Satan and sadly, some accept this statement as truth because it gives them something to "know" which they believe others do not know. This is one of many actions which God categorizes as "pride" and brings God's wrath down upon those who engage in such an activity.

Scripture clearly speaks of **the Bride of Christ as those souls who God is developing here on earth. They are a people who love God, give of themselves to learn of Him, and strive to be a worthy bride for Christ by keeping His statutes.**

To say that Christ was married to Mary Magdalene, in light of what scripture tells us, implies that a *divorce* would have to take place between Christ and Mary Magdalene before Christ could accept *the Bride* God has chosen for Him. Scripture *clearly* tells us that Christ *and his Bride* will reign together during the Thousand Year Kingdom of Peace and again in the Holy City of God for all eternity.

Scripture also teaches that the Father, the Son and the Holy Spirit are one, are a Trinity, thus what one does affects the others. The hierarchy of this

Trinity becomes clear as we learn through scripture that Christ always defers to His Father. When we read how Christ prays, we see that His prayers end with the words "Thy will be done, not mine."

When Christ prayed in the Garden of Gethsemane before He was to die on the cross, He asked God to take that cup away from Him but then closed His prayer to His Father with the words *"not my will but Thy will be done."* The closeness of this relationship would indicate that Christ would have discussed any marriage with His Father. With God in the process of preparing a "bride" for His Son, God could never have agreed to such a union, nor to a divorce which would negate many of God's statutes and *break the faith of generations of Christians to come.*

Therefore when someone makes the claim that Christ and Mary Magdalene married, it demonstrates their lack of knowledge about Christianity and about the scriptures. It shows that they place their faith into what is written by man into a book or documentary obviously inspired by Satan and fully negated in the Holy Scriptures!

Revelation 14:15 tells us that there is a special "time" when God's Plan will be complete. The highlight of God's Plan is when He sends Christ back to earth for the First Resurrection to "reap the harvest" of His huge investment in mankind. This verse says: *".....Thrust in thy sickle and reap: for the time is come for thee to reap; for the harvest of the earth is ripe."*

Revelation 19:7 gives us insight into what this harvest is by telling us: *"Let us be glad and rejoice, and give honour to him;* **<u>for the marriage of the Lamb</u>** **(Christ)** *<u>is come, and his wife</u>* **<u>(the children of God)</u>** *<u>hath made herself ready.</u>"*

There are another two verses applicable to those who say Jesus was married to Mary Magdalene.

These are found at the very end of the Bible and refer to everything relating to God's Plan of Salvation and what He teaches us through scripture. Revelation 22: 18, 19 states: *"If anyone adds to these things, God will add to him the plagues which are written in this book; and if anyone takes away from the words of the book of this prophecy,* **God shall take away his part from the Book of Life, from the holy city, and from the things which are written in this book.**

Will we be ready for this harvest? Will we be counted as worthy to become a part of God's people and a part of the Bride of Christ? Or will we be lost for our "lack of knowledge?

We can never learn enough. Scripture explains that after the Thousand Year Kingdom of Peace, Satan, his fallen angels and the people who scripture calls the "goats" will be bound in the Lake of Fire and forgotten. Like the five foolish virgins many of the "goats" will be stunned to find themselves cast out of the community of God. They will have an eternity to commiserate over their loss and to look back on the many opportunities God gave them to come under His blessing *and they refused to do so.*

The "First Resurrection" signifies joyous immortality and the "Resurrection of the Damned" signifies a tormented immortality. If we look at this from the time described in the first four verses of Revelation 20, the period during which Satan is bound, and the thousand year reign has commenced, the unjust who have to appear at the judgment seat of Christ will have been *"punished with everlasting destruction and **banished from the presence of the Lord**, and from the glory of his power,"* which is the second death. When those deemed "the goats" who are those with a lack of knowledge, **those who did not care to learn or to practice God's statutes** are thrown into the Lake of Fire, they will be forgotten; they will no longer have *"a portion in anything that is done under the sun."*

We all need God to open our understanding so we can be successful in developing a true relationship with Him. God knows how easily we fall into complacency, but He looks at our heart and our striving and forgives our misdeeds **if we make the effort to learn of Him, love Him and follow Him.** God looks for us to understand His plan and the rules of righteousness under which He must labour so we can bring testimony to others; help others find their way to God. Thus God warns us that a "lack of knowledge" may become the stumbling block which prevents our growth and ability to be a part of the first resurrection. Adding anything to scripture which does not belong there is dangerous and could cost us our soul salvation.

The final battle between good and evil is explained quite vividly throughout scripture. Many poignant verses about this subject can be found in Revelation 16:14, 16, in Daniel 2:44, Revelation 19:11-16, 21, Ezekiel 39:7 and 17-20 and many other places throughout scripture. **This final battle between good and evil is a time of great suffering for**

mankind. It will last for three and one half years. It will include earthquakes, floods, lightning, fire and brimstone from the air, plagues, famine, pestilence, a fire so great that men's flesh will burn, and so many other horrors that it is hard to imagine. It is a war beyond imagination. In fact scripture provides an imagery so precise that we almost cringe just reading about what will occur.

Those who Christ will take are described in Revelation 20:6: *"**Blessed and holy is he that hath part in the first resurrection: on such the second death hath no power**, but they shall be priests of God and of Christ, and shall reign with him a thousand years."* And in Revelation 3:21 God tells us:*"To him that overcometh, will I grant to sit with me in my throne, even as I also overcame, and am set down with my Father in his throne."* Revelation 12:12 warns: *"Woe to the inhabitants of the earth and the sea."*

Many have questions about what the sea might hold which will face God's wrath.(It is interesting to note that many UFO sightings and actual photographs demonstrate that flying objects often rise from or descend into the sea.)Scripture itself addresses the dead who are raised from the sea for the First Resurrection. *"And the sea gave up the dead which were in it; and death and hell delivered up the dead which were in them: and **they were judged** every man according to their works."* (Revelation 20:13)

In Philip 3:11, the Apostle Paul says:*"If by any means I might attain unto the resurrection of the dead."* And in Acts 24:15 says: *"...there shall be a resurrection of the dead: both of the just and unjust"*. Paul's desire was to reach the First Resurrection, be a part of the Bride of Christ, and return with Christ after the "wedding feast in Heaven" for the reign of the Thousand Years of Peace when all will bow to Christ and believe. This goal should also live in our hearts!

It is in harmony with this use of the "resurrection," that Jesus says in John 5:29: *"They that have done good (shall come forth) unto the resurrection of life, and they that have done evil (shall come forth) unto the resurrection of damnation."* It is important to note that a lack of interest and effort is considered a part of the evil or the "Adam-like nature" which cannot enter God's new kingdom. God seeks those who develop a Christ-like nature.

The *"resurrection of life"* to which the righteous come forth from earth and from their graves offers us the gift of living with Christ for all eternity in peace and joy. The *"resurrection of damnation"* to which the unrighteous will come from their graves, brings these souls to judgment and then to the second death which will imprison them in torment as a punishment. The resurrection of the righteous precludes the "reigning" with Christ a thousand years when every soul, living or dead will know Christ and God's Plan of Salvation

Thus the word "resurrection" denotes a state or condition, which is confirmed in the verse found in Revelations 20:6: *"Blessed and holy is he that hath part in the **first** resurrection: on such, the second* *death hath no power."* The "second death" is the consummation of the punishment which will be inflicted on the unrighteous, and is, therefore, the conclusion of the resurrection of damnation.

Those who come forth to the resurrection **of life** will not be subjected to the second death, and hence the state of things in which they have a part or portion is appropriately called "the **first** resurrection."

Our attempts to understand scripture demonstrates that we have much to learn; that we need God to open our understanding so we can put together His plan of Salvation and strive harder to be pleasing to him. We also need to understand God's plan so that we can bring testimony to others; help others find their way to God. Therefore God's words which warn us that a "lack of knowledge" may become the stumbling block which prevents our growth and ability to be a part of the first resurrection should not be taken lightly.

What God describes in scripture about the end time destruction is not something anyone would choose to live through yet the **_only_** way we can avoid these events lies in our being taken up with Christ at the first resurrection. Those who will **not** be a part of the first resurrection, **not** be a part of the Bride of Christ, will have to endure incredible suffering and incredible fear....so great in fact that men will call out to die. They will experience what scripture refers to as "Armageddon", a war and a destruction which will encompass the entire earth. (Jeremiah 25:32-34).

The final battle between good and evil is explained quite vividly throughout scripture. Many poignant verses are found in Revelation 16:14, 16, in Daniel 2:44, Revelation 19:11-16, 21, Ezekiel 39:7 and 17-20 and many other places throughout scripture. **This final battle between good and evil is a time of great suffering for mankind. It will last for three and one half years.** It will include earthquakes, floods, lightning, fire and brimstone from the air, plagues, famine, pestilence, a fire so great that men's flesh will burn, and so many other horrors that it is hard to imagine. It is a war beyond imagination for which scripture provides an imagery so precise that we almost cringe just reading about what will occur.

Satan and all things evil will bring the fullness of their resources against God and against God's people and it will be a terrible time for the earth. A great mountain will fall into the sea, the sea will turn red, one third of all men will die, one third of all fish will die, great turbulences in the weather will frighten mankind and many other horrors will occur during this time of spiritual warfare.

Thus, we do not want to be counted with those who have a lack of knowledge about God's Plan of Salvation or among those who cannot escape this destruction. But rather we want to be a part of the first resurrection where we can be with Christ until the destruction ends and Christ returns to earth with us; with His Bride, to establish peace and a sin free world.

Those who Christ will take are described in Revelation 20:6: *"Blessed and holy is he that hath part in the first resurrection: on such the second death hath no power, but they shall be priests of God and of Christ, and shall reign with him a thousand years."*

And in Revelation 3:21 God tells us: *"To him that overcometh, will I grant to sit with me in my throne, even as I also overcame, and am set down with my Father in his throne."*

These souls will not be affected when Satan is again released "for a little while" after the thousand years of peace, only those not yet tested, those born during this period of time, and those remaining in eternity.

Chapter Eight

ALIENS & DECLASSIFICATION

How can our faith possibly accept the idea that aliens exist, that UFO's fly freely over this earth, that photographs and eye witness accounts exist to support these claims? How can we reconcile this information with what we read in scripture and what we have believed all this time? What if there _is_ scripture that hints at this phenomenon?

The declassification of UFO documentation began in the United Kingdom in 2008. According to Wikipedia, Russia, Equador, France, Denmark, Brazil, Sweden, Canada, the United States and many other countries followed that decision during 2009. New Zealand released their information in 2010. Scientists are comparing the information from all these countries in an effort to learn from it. On January 20, 2017, 12 million pages of CIA files became available for study online. They were released under the Freedom of Information Act and in many cases note the size, colour, sound, unusual features and actions which many eye witnesses gave of UFO sightings.

Some of this information goes back to 1940 and not only includes eye witness accounts, but also drawings, photograph, videos, and in a few cases actual parts of what they described. The eye witnesses were comprised of well respected people, many in the armed forces who were on ships or planes at the time. A fair question to ask is why is this information just now being declassified? Automatic declassification occurs when a certain predetermined time frame has expired which is often 25 years. However, if the information could damage our national security it is often not released to the public and becomes "exempt" from the automatic declassification time frame. Classified records are kept in the National Archives of the NARA Federal Records centers in specially designated locations of the Department of Justice. They are released to enhance the knowledge of the general public, researchers, institutions, and for historical purposes.

Amazingly, most of the information about aliens and UFO's are incredibly similar whether a sighting took place in Norway, Spain, The United States, or any other location.

God's emphasis on fear fits perfectly into what some may feel about their faith when confronted with information they'd never before considered.

Now, as new information is released which could truly challenge what was considered an established religious belief, we must move carefully. Most of all we must study scripture with a new perspective to see if God has indeed provided the information we need in scripture and is something which we have simply not viewed with an eye toward this phenomenon thus have not fully understood.

We must maintain our faith despite information which can shake our original concept of the world as we have perceived it. We must pray and ask God to open our understanding and help us through new disclosures which demand answers. We must also beware the new religions which have developed as a result of this information and are filled with false prophets and satanic deception. We must continue to trust God as we have done in the past.

With an open mind and heart many have taken a new look at the hieroglyphics found in the ruins of ancient civilizations noting that some appear to depict the shapes we now call "Flying Saucers" or "UFO's". Other drawings and carvings appear to depict large men wearing what looks very similar to the space suits and helmets with which we are familiar. As we study these hieroglyphics and stone carvings and compare these to the recent disclosure of classified information we can see a marked resemblance. Can we fit this information into our concept of God's Plan of Salvation? Or......will scripture open up more of its mysteries so we can see that God purposely planned for what we are just now learning?

Could these "aliens" be a part of the Nephilim race destroyed through the flood? Or are these beings another type of angel sent to earth by God to help mankind move forward in their technology and development *or are they the fallen angels who joined Satan to bring harm to mankind and destroy their faith in God?*

These questions can place a number of concerns into our hearts and clearly demonstrates that perhaps we need to re-think the narrowness of the faith we have embraced. Perhaps we need to be more open to a ***universe*** which God controls rather than just our limited earth which still holds many of its secrets. Is it time for us to widen our horizons and accept that there are more aspects to God's activities than we've realized?

As we look back at the Garden of Eden and the flora and fauna which God showed Adam and Eve we learn through scripture the diversity in God's creation. It is through the creation that God began the miracle of teaching us of His power and majesty and showing us what lives in His heart and what He wishes us to learn. Every diverse part of the creation, God saw as good. (Genesis 1:10)

Scripture tells us that our Heavenly Father brought into being many grasses, seeds, and fruit trees, which He also saw as good. (Genesis 1:11-12) And when everything God created for our benefit was in place, Genesis 1:31 tells us that He considered it **all** "very good"! To discern what God seeks to teach us through His creation we must first recognize that what God so lovingly created was incredibly diverse. He designed birds to be magnificently different in shape and size and color, in song and flight. He designed trees of every size; tall and small, thin and wide, some with fruit and some without, some with needles and some with leaves. The leaves were of every shape and size and many changed with the seasons.

He designed the seas to be calm **_and_** stormy, thus both serene and frightening, He designed the skies to hold clouds of every size and shape which move slowly or quickly depending upon the changing winds. When we study what God created and seek to learn from it, we learn that He is not only providing for us materially, but also spiritually. The diversity of His creation teaches us to view not only the differences in birds and animals, flora and fauna as beautiful and beneficial, but also to appreciate the differences in mankind as well. He wants us to view those differences through His eyes. He is teaching us through His creation. Perhaps we are now entering a new era where we are ready to learn more about God's creations; learn the incredible diversity which exists in the entire universe.

In Genesis 2:8 we read: *"And the Lord God planted a garden eastward in Eden and there He put the man whom He had formed."* The creation can teach us what God planted and why. For example, God created some flowers for their immediate beauty which quickly draws us to them. Through this we are made ready to acknowledge the beauty and generosity in God's heart. But our Heavenly Father also planted many other flowers in the garden, some not as beautiful, but each to bring us a valuable lesson.

Some flowers were created to have great strength as an example of endurance. Some were created for their exquisite aroma which God likens to our offerings. (Genesis 8:21, Ephesians 5:2) Some flowers were created with dense foliage to prevent another from robbing them of their place in the garden, which teach us to fill ourselves with God's words so we do not allow evil to rob us of our place in Heaven.

Others reach out from their planting with a delicately cascading grace showing us that we too must reach out to others with the offer of God's grace. Some flowers may not offer a surface beauty yet provide great value because God implanted within them the ability to heal through their medicinal components. This teaches us that God wants to heal us so we can heal others.

God's garden clearly demonstrates that though flowers are different, one flower is not "better" than another. Each has a place in God's garden and each can proclaim the value God gave them when He created them. Though different, though their value is sometimes hidden, God created them for and with a purpose and He wants them to fulfill that purpose. Thus everything God created was good, everything worked together in harmony, and was equally blessed.

But when sin entered the world the blessing was lost and a curse came upon the entire creation whereby thorns and weeds began to overpower what was good and beautiful. What had once worked in harmony began to fall into disharmony. Suddenly, under the curse, one flower began to overpower another. One flower grew so tall that it stole the sun from another. One flower grew deeper roots to steal water from its neighbor. One plant began to demand and create an alkaline soil, while another demanded an acid soil. Some became poisonous, hiding their venomous nature under the guise of their beauty. The flowers had fallen under the curse of sin and were transformed. This tells us that the curse of sin can poison our soul.

People are much the same. They are as different as the flowers in God's garden. Just as He did with the flowers, God purposely created differences in people to teach us the joy and harmony which can exist in a unique and varied creation. He wants us to appreciate what He created; to learn the value of each difference, and to respect that each has equal value in His eyes. Thus, while we are different from one another; each of us has great value; **equal** value. We lose that blessing however when we do not do as God asks and do not heed the warnings God provides for us.

God's children must understand that we are to celebrate our differences and learn from them; that we are to fight against and even flee from those who, under the curse of evil, begin to hate, discriminate, and bring harm. God wants us to appreciate what we have and what we are, rather than envy those who we foolishly believe are more or better. We are not to hate or fear those who we falsely believe are less or inferior. Appreciation for what we have rather than what we want is an important aspect of being content. *Appreciation for* *others* *touches God's heart.* Thus perhaps a willingness to accept another aspect of God's creation is now what we are to learn.

Thus, just like the flowers, God has created people who are different from one another; some with black hair, some brown hair, and some with blonde hair. He has created us with brown skin and black skin, white skin and yellow skin, red skin, and almost everything in between. He has created people who are tall and short, stocky and thin, with brown eyes or amber eyes, blue eyes or hazel eyes. Some may smile while others frown. Some need attention and others prefer to stay in the shadows, But just as Satan entered God's garden to interject thorns and weeds and poisons to pervert the plants, so has he entered man to pervert them to pride, arrogance, self-satisfaction, envy, hatred, racism, a sense of superiority or inferiority. Through our sin and complacency Satan can work to destroy our understanding that God created and loves the diversity in man just as He created and loves the diversity in nature. *Each flower and each person is equal to another through the very uniqueness God granted them.* Thus perhaps we are to learn that **angels are also diverse, also to be loved and** *appreciated, also to be a part of God's eternal family.*

God also created our ability to love, to hope, to trust, and to develop a special talent which He hopes we will nurture and use in His service. Despite our failures, God wants us to put aside the Adam-like nature which accepted sin and negated diversity and develop the Christ-like nature which fights sin and appreciates our diversity. *Free will allows us to decide which attitude and which nature we will embrace.* Free will allows us to decide to be thankful and loving or choose to be angry and hateful. Free will *forces us* to take responsibility for our choices. It is up to us what those choices bring into our lives, and what they will ultimately mean to God and to our soul salvation. Free will allows us to decide to accept what may be a new era of discovery and build our faith, trust and acceptance of God's Plan rather than diminish.

Scripture teaches us that, through prayer, God helps us recognize what our mistakes have been and to carefully consider the beam in our own eye rather than the speck in our brother's eye. (Matthew 7:3) *"Why beholdest thou the mote that is in thy brothers eye but consider not the beam that is in thine own eye?"*

God encourages us to choose the path of love and peace and joy rather than the path of hate, anxiety, anger and judgment which comes from evil. Evil is always angry and cunning, sly and envious, plotting and malicious, jealous and unappreciative. Evil makes us proud and haughty, self-serving and unloving. Evil creates racism and self importance. Evil invokes fear in our hearts to break our faith. Evil makes us so arrogant that we see no need to learn of God or act on what we learn. God tells us that *Pride goeth before a fall!*

But righteousness makes us happy and honest, open and supportive, appreciative and humble, giving and loving. Righteousness removes fear and hate and envy and replaces it with peace and love. Righteousness causes us to esteem others higher than ourselves. Righteousness shows us our sin and our separation from God,

Sometimes we may wish that we were a different flower in God's garden, but we must remember that we **are** one of God's flowers and He asks that we appreciate *where* He placed us. God gave us our personal attributes because He plans to use them in His new kingdom if we have been found worthy to be there. He offers us grace so our sins do not prevent our worthiness but only when we have sought that grace. God wants us to develop the gifts He gave us and become the best we can be. Through God, through our appreciative heart and the forgiveness of sin, we can find righteousness and joy…. and a great satisfaction in what and who we are no matter where we find ourselves planted. All gifts await us as the Bride of Christ because each of us will be a part of the garden God planted just for her!

Just as a flower will balk at being planted in a less than perfect environment, we may occasionally think that we are not where we should be or even that God's plan is not what we expected. We must remember however, that God never makes a mistake and therefore, we have been beautifully created, are planted where we can grow, and God's plan is perfect! It is through God's love that we can be nourished and grow stronger in the environment in which we find ourselves. It is how we learn that *our happiness should not be tied to material possessions,* beauty, talent, the temporal, or what we expected, but tied only to the heart and the amount and purity of love it holds. Happiness is being a part of God's family.

Let us not be those who listen to the whispers of Satan and weaken and die in sin but those who grow in strength and love to bloom in the Son! Therefore, as we read of new discoveries, read newly released documents, or watch a television show which recounts the classified information now released, we need not be afraid. We can look forward to a new and exciting part of God's Plan of Salvation and build our faith to even greater heights.

Thus, while many countries release what was once classified UFO information dating back to the 1940's we can listen with excitement to what God is revealing. We need not be concerned to learn for example, that Norway lists an episode in Mountain Farm near Torpo on July 16, 1986, another in Hordland on April 12, 1997, another in Trysil on January 2, 2010 and in Hessdalen village on April 16, 2016 which were all very similar. The latest sighting as this book was being written was on May 20, 2017.

Most of the sightings are very similar to one another even though from such varied parts of the world. Thus we must seriously consider that one of the classes of angels mentioned in scripture are called the "Thrones" or "Wheels" who have many eyes with which to watch the earth and navigate God's chariots. If we imagine what the angels called "Wheels" may look like, and imagine them carrying God's chariots, we can compare this biblical description to the UFO's being described by many eye witnesses and photos.

In most cases, the UFO's were said to be very large round discs or spheroids. They displayed lights circling their outer rim. They move at speeds so fast they baffled even the pilots and astronauts who reported the sighting and took photographs. They are said to move straight up or down, right or left, backward and forward and can even hover. They have often been seen entering the sea at an incredible speed and angle. One report dated July 7, 1948 states that a UFO crashed and was taken to the military base in San Antonio. The UFO was measured as 90 feet across, silver in color disc-shaped, and first seen 30 miles south southwest of Laredo, Texas.

There have even been reports of "beings" seen through the windows of the UFO's and the United States claims to have the body of at least one of these creatures from outer space as well as one of the UFO's themselves. From NASA employees to Radar technicians, from Police Officers to Defense Contractors, From Astronauts to Pilots and even via groups of people sightings have been reported for years. Such renowned people as Gordon Cooper, USAF pilot and NASA Astronaut; Edgar Mitchell, Apollo Astronaut; Admiral Rosco Hillenkoetter; President Harry Truman; President Jimmy Carter; General Douglas MacArthur, Dr. James McDonald, Professor of Atmospheric Sciences, UFO's; Lord Downing, Air Chief Marshall; General Nathan Twining, Joint Chief of Staff; Dr, Herman Oberthand many, many others have attested to, even documented similar sightings.

But there is also another consideration as we read in scripture that Abaddon will rise from the "Abyss". Interestingly the "Abyss" is what the fourth level of the ocean is called. It is located from 13,124 feet to 19,686 feet below sea level according to the Sea and Sky website on the Internet. This website provides a diagram of the sea levels listing the first from the surface of the earth down to 656 feet as the Epipelagic (sunlight) zone. The website adds that the Mesopelagic (twilight) zone exists from 656 feet to 3,300 feet below sea level, the Bathypelagic (midnight) zone which Sperm whales can reach carries a water pressure of 5850 pounds per square inch and exists from 3281 feet to 13,124 feet below sea level. The Abyssopelagic Zone or the "Abyss" exists from 13,124 to 19,686 feet below sea level and makes up ¾ of the oceans depth. The final zone, the Hadalpelagic Zone, also known as the Trenches exists between 19,686 to 35,787 feet below sea level in which starfish and tube worms can exist.

We know that scripture contains mysteries which God opens to mankind as it is needed and as those with pure seeking hearts ask God to do so. Therefore it may be time for us to research scripture even further and do our best to learn what God wants to tell us about this phenomenon and the end times we still face.

Chapter Nine

THE "MYSTERY" OF SCRIPTURE

What we can glean from the previous chapters is that God's Plan for Mankind has spanned far more "time" than we can even imagine and that it is far more complex than we originally understood.

From just the few passages of scripture which have been shown to divulge information heretofor apparently undiscovered, we can see that there is much more for us to learn from God's words. Added to this is the incredible complexity of our human nature and how our DNA works to create the individual characteristics we claim as "good" or "bad". Amazingly, scripture even addresses the emotional state of man and warns us that Satan can completely override our common sense and create havoc and unbelief in our lives.

Evidently, through all the information scripture provides, God is telling us that none of us can *prevent* the attributes we inherit but that *we can control them* through the application of God's word. This control gives the child of God the title of "overcomer" to whom much is promised! It helps immensely to know what to expect and trust to obtain a satisfying outcome.

Most of us easily understand our response to physical pain, but do not fully understand our response to either emotional pain or the pain of thought in opposition to the word of God. These emotional discomforts are those we usually try to hide. These emotions can reside in our soul as a form of guilt but also as an impetus to continue in our sins and feel that we need not move closer to God.

Our earlier discussion of the giants who roamed the earth before the flood and were produced from the union of a fallen angel with a human woman should alert us to the fact that through the genes we receive, we develop certain proclivities. This falls neatly into what scripture tells us about "inherited sin" which also plays a role in our own growth and development.

Yet scripture tells us in Romans 8:28, *"All things work together for the good of those that love the Lord,* and therefore we think that we must wear a happy face regardless of how or why we suffer inside and what we try to hide or what we fear.

Those words do teach us however that the children of God are aware that while Satan revels in our heartache, our fear and our guilt, our Heavenly

Father in His loving kindness and the righteousness under which He works, wants to turn all these negative emotions and proclivities into a blessing.

However, because of sin, our Heavenly Father has ordained that our lives be a training ground whereby we learn how to become all that God wants in the Bride for His Son. God wants us to overcome those things which emanate from evil and work to destroy our relationship with God.

God allows difficult circumstances to exist in our lives and touch our heart deeply so *they can become a marker of our character development and of the overcoming capacity* of those called to be the Bride of Christ. Nevertheless, there are times when we live through circumstances or witness circumstances occurring in our lives and in the lives of those we love, that we ask ourselves privately how this promise of good from all circumstances could be possible.

Even though we believe that scripture is God's personal, accurate and irrefutable instruction, seldom do we think to ask Him to unravel the mystery attached to His words and help us recognize their miracle. We seldom tell Him that we sometimes struggle to understand how to apply His words. Often we are embarrassed to share with others the thoughts and fears we have because we do not want to be seen as weak in faith. We suffer in silence and do not admit that inwardly we rail at what we face and then feel guilty about our private thoughts.

Sometimes we fully recognize that we are by nature lackadaisical and complacent about our faith. We don't always strive to have a true relationship with God and haven't the drive to learn and do as God asks. But God, in His loving kindness provides us with information which tells us of our fate if we continue in this state of complacency. And, of course, He offers grace.

God also teaches us the difference between what we can allow ourselves to feel and what we should struggle *against* feeling. As we examine scripture, we learn that the *expression* of the fear, pain, guilt or sorrow we experience is best understood as we examine what Christ lived through and what **He** felt and expressed.

Christ's reaction as he prayed just before His day of agony on the cross should be our example. Christ spoke the words to His Father: *"Take away this cup from me"*.

This tells us that we should not feel guilty if we ask God to change our circumstances. God wants us to be open with Him, to express our fears and our wants and desires in the deep and personal communication of our prayers.

As Christ prayed before His death on the cross, the love in His heart and the trust He had in His Father allowed Him to submit to the sacrifice He was to make *for us* and demonstrate the character in His soul which then caused Him to utter the words, *"Nevertheless, not what I will, but what thou will"*.

These words are our example and from them we can know with certainty that God allows us to express our fear and the pain we feel, and even to wish that our circumstances were different. It is not that we are judged and found lacking if we ask God to take our troubles away, but that we *end up accepting* God's will and doing our best to use those circumstances to prove our character. Our troubles will then produce an indicator of the trust and acceptance we have developed regarding the decisions of our Heavenly Father. It demonstrates what has grown in our heart ….no matter what circumstances we face.

How we handle our weaknesses becomes, in essence, a marker of our spiritual maturity. The miracle which occurs when we **adjust** our thoughts and actions..... as Christ did when facing His heartrending circumstances..... is that once we submit to God's will, often our heartaches become easier to bear or simply disappear. In fact, even our complacency can change if we ask God to help us overcome our failures.

Once Satan realizes he cannot break our faith, nor break our trust, nor prevent the change we seek for our lives, there is no reason for him to continue his harassment. We can therefore be released from Satan's captivity because we have demonstrated that we are wiser and more trustworthy for having mastered the test which these circumstances brought us. This was what occurred with Job.

Certainly it is difficult to experience heartache, disappointment, fear, or failure. Certainly it is difficult to have to defend our hard earned faith when it is under assault. Nevertheless, we should examine Christ's plea that God remove the cup from which He was to drink and recognize His humanity through His prayers.

Mark 14:34 tells us of the emotional pain Christ suffered: *"My soul is exceedingly sorrowful unto death."* Mark 14:36 tells us that when Christ prayed, He said, *"Abba Father, all things are possible unto thee. Take away this cup from me, nevertheless not what I will but what thou will."*

What few of us realize is that Christ later **repeated** this plea. Asking God a second time *and a third time* was indicative of how much He was suffering as he thought of what was to come. Mark 14:39 tells us, *"and again He went away and prayed, and spoke the same words."*

Therefore, if we are caught up in a difficult circumstance, we need not feel guilty when we ask God to let our circumstances pass...or change..... as long as our heart truly desires that God's will be paramount. Such a response is indicative of the trust we place in God's design for our lives.

This advice also applies to the assault on our faith or our long held belief system. Trying to be more introspective and asking ourselves if we trust that what is occurring is for our good is pleasing to God.. Desiring to accept what God has willed in order to develop our character and eliminate all evil, helps us grow into the Bride God desires for His Son.

Once we reflect on these questions and ask our Heavenly Father to help us *learn* from everything we experience, we can move with all our heart and with great sincerity from the words *"Take this away"* to the words, *"Thy will be done"*. This allows God access to our hearts to help us create the change in us we require.

Our character.....which is comprised of our ability to love and forgive, to have compassion and understanding, **to submit to God's will,** to be loyal and to trust God implicitly..... will be measured by how we deal with our circumstances....especially when our faith is challenged.

Those who have developed these attributes will be a part of the five wise, and not the five foolish virgins, and found worthy to go with the Lord when He takes His Bride.

All that we will learn of God's Plan of Salvation and all our questions about why God exercised His will as He did, still point to our job to trust that it was done for our greater good. How we handle our fear, our doubt, our concerns and our failures will be an example to those around us.

How well we can accept what we may feel is the true marker of our spiritual maturity and God always creates a blessing from our heartache proving that all things work for the good of those who love the Lord.

Christ dreaded the circumstances which He was to live through. He was afraid. He found Himself without any earthly support, and without a true and loyal friend. Christ's cup was a bitter one; it was the most bitter cup of circumstances we could ever imagine, yet because of His love for us, He stood firm, and He trusted and **obeyed** what His Heavenly Father ordained.

Satan threw everything he had against Christ, but Christ remained stedfast. Thus, the Bride of Christ must remain firm in her trust and obedience to God and bring her sorrow, fear and doubt to God with a pure and honest heart.

It's okay to tell our Heavenly Father that we are tired, that we feel saddened by our circumstances, that we feel that we can no longer carry our cross or that we are afraid because of the doubt which can creep into our heart. God understands and He too feels sorrow, but looks (as we should) to the end result of His Plan of Salvation and the end result of our commitment to God.

But in the end, we can rest assured that God loves us. God sees our tears and carries us through all circumstances. And then, when we finally accept His will and **_His_** way of achieving success, He creates a blessing from our circumstances. And He opens the mystery of scripture to us to help us remain firm in faith.

Most of us feel incredible awe when we recognize the wondrous love God has for us and from that love, sent His Son that we might be ransomed from sin. These are the greatest gifts we could ever ask for; they are priceless....they are incredible treasures. In addition to these treasures,

God has provided us with yet another gift which assists those who seek Him with an open heart. It is meant to help us fully understand His plan of salvation. It is *the gift of scripture* and teaches us everything we need to know to reach the goal of our faith.

Prayer is another wonderful gift which gives us strength and God clearly tells us in Matthew 18:20: *"For where two or three are gathered together in my name, there am I in the midst of them."* There is then a blessing when husbands and wives (and others) pray aloud together.

Scripture teaches us of the beauty and goodness which lives in the heart of God and demonstrates His emotion, His love, His goals, His plan, His desire, His righteousness, and His power. Scripture also teaches us about God's enemy, why that enemy seeks the destruction of our faith, and how we can protect ourselves from that destruction. Scripture teaches us how to love and how we are to treat one another and through that love, become worthy to spend eternity with Him and His Son.

None of us want our children to marry someone abusive or someone who thrives on contention. We want them to marry someone who can love and be kind, be empathetic and godly; someone who can be a role model. Similarly, our Heavenly Father seeks those who employ their free will to become a people who **choose** to have a relationship with God, who **choose** to love, who **choose** to be kind and loyal, who **choose** honor and integrity for all facets of their lives, and who **choose** to spurn all things evil.

Our Heavenly Father wants love and righteousness to reign in the new heaven and earth and He graciously provides us with everything we need so we can become all He desires. Scripture is one of our best teaching tools, and when we seek to understand what God wants to tell us, and do so with an open heart, all is revealed to us as our understanding grows ....if we are *willing* to learn.

If we attempt to teach an infant how to make a bed, we soon learn that they cannot yet accomplish this goal. If we try to teach a child to solve a complex physics problem, we may also learn that without a background in math they may not solve the problem. But when the children grow, and have been taught the proper basic instruction to prepare them for more complex tasks, they can learn, and in time can accomplish more than they could earlier in life.

Similarly as God's children, we come to Him as infants in need of instruction. We must learn to bring a willing heart to the goal of learning and then trust what we are taught. We must apply ourselves to becoming all that God knows we **can** become. As our understanding is opened, our trust increases, and God sees when we are ready for Him to provide us with the fullness of His blessing....one of which is to help us understand scripture. Our fears can be allayed through this knowledge.

One of the fascinating components of scripture is that while its wisdom is easily read and understood by many, it is ***clearly hidden from others***. The children of God learn that amazingly more is revealed as we grow in faith. It is our honest seeking and our faith which allows the Holy Spirit to open the secrets of scripture to those who seek to learn with a humble heart and those who commit themselves to a true relationship with God.

The Holy Spirit provides what we need at just the right time to those who have been "made ready" to understand and accept and believe the deepest elements of scripture. This is called the "mystery" of the Bible and is another component which demonstrates how much God loves us, protects us, and guides our steps toward a perfect understanding. King David, despite his many faults and failings, loved God so deeply that he could always touch God's heart. He communed with God through prayer and he trusted God with his life. David said in Psalms 18:28, *"For thou wilt light our candle: The Lord my God will enlighten my darkness."* This was a plea from David to God asking for a greater understanding, and a request that he be given the fire of motivation to live a more godly life in the future. His use of the word "will" indicates the trust he had that God would provide him with that enlightenment.

Matthew 13:11 teaches us that understanding the things of God is a mystery **not understood by everyone**. *"Because it is given unto you to know the mysteries of the kingdom of heaven, but to them it is not given."* Further along in that chapter in Matthew we learn that not all who see or hear will accept what God teaches....or offers. We also learn that God can open our understanding if we ask Him to do this and are willing to do what God asks of us. Luke 24:31 tells us, *"And their eyes were opened, and they knew him....."*

Sadly, some arrogantly believe that they already know all there is to know. This attitude can shortchange one's spiritual growth and is a trap laid by Satan to prevent us from fully maturing in our faith. Others feel that they need only go to church, tithe and have their sins forgiven. But scripture teaches us so much more. It addresses how we are to treat one another; how we are to pray; what kind of a relationship we should seek with God; what God seeks for His new kingdom and why!

All of us, whether we feel that we already know what our faith dictates, or whether we feel that scripture is too difficult to fully understand, should pray and ask God to continue to teach us and continue to place in our hearts and souls all that we need to learn and do to please Him.

We need to ask God to **continuously** enlighten us so that we can be open to where God wants to lead us, and protected from the complacency Satan has planted in so many hearts. Complacency was why the five foolish virgins were left behind. As the Holy Spirit fills us, we will be liberated from the spirits of this world who want us bound and kept from the fullness of God's truths.

As mentioned above, Matthew 13:11 tells us *"Because it is given unto you to **know the mysteries** of the Kingdom of Heaven, but to them it is not given."* This verse clearly defines two different groups of people; those who actively seek to learn and those who do not. It explains we can only grow in our faith through learning God's words and receive the gift of understanding.

Conversely, **not** learning God's words will block our understanding, thus block our spiritual growth. This contributes to confusion about the meaning of scripture and blocks the blessing of knowledge. Hosea 4:6 warns: *"My people are destroyed for lack of knowledge: because thou hast rejected knowledge, **I will also reject thee**....."*

This verse clearly tells us that God wants us to learn so we can prepare for the new heaven and earth He is preparing which will be free of all things evil. Thus only a people who will spurn evil and freely desire and follow what is righteous in God's eyes will be allowed to enter. Pride and arrogance, a lack of knowledge and no true relationship with our Heavenly Father and with the Bridegroom of our soul will cause us to be denied entrance into God's new kingdom.

Thus we must make ourselves ready for this transition. We must grow from child to adult, from the Adam-like nature to the Christ-like nature, from being unable to recognize evil, to easily discerning evil, and **from complacency about evil to a warrior laboring to overcome evil.**

Scripture does not change, but hopefully we do. By giving our hearts and lives to God, by striving to do His will, by loving one another, and by praying for enlightenment, God will open the mysteries and truths of scripture to us. May each of us grow in Spirit so we can learn, and make of ourselves all that our Heavenly Father wants us to be!

And finally, as we learned in Chapter 2, there are **but a few _very_ important words** found in Genesis which teaches us how evolution and creation work hand in hand. Yet this information seemed "hidden" as evidenced by those who claimed that the Theory of Evolution could not exist with the Theory of Creation. This is a perfect example of how the "mystery" of scripture unfolds. This is a perfect example of how God provides everything we need to know through scripture.

Additional examples of a mystery yet to be solved are found in Ecclesiastes 21:3 which speaks of a "time" for everything in God's plan. This may explain why Satan is loosed again for "a season" after the Thousand Years of Peace. But in the Book of Enoch Chapter 21 (This book was taken out of the Apocrypha but can be found as a translation by R.H. Charles at www.scaredtexts.org.) tells us that Uriel the Archangel explained Enoch's vision of a spectacle of pain for the fallen angels. Uriel assured Enoch that the fallen angels would spend 10,000 years in the Lake of fire but then be transported somewhere even worse for their *eternal* imprisonment.

In terms of the final judgment and the hell which will become the future for the fallen angels **and for those of mankind who did not accept God thus would not practice His admonitions,** we also read in scripture in Revelation 20:13-15: *"And **the sea** gave up the dead which were in it; and death and hell delivered up the dead which were in them; and they were judged.....and death and hell were cast into the Lake of fire. This is the second death. And whosoever was not found written in the book of life was cast into the lake of fire."*

The sea giving up its dead may even reference the UFO's which were photographed so often as exiting and entering the sea. Thus the full mystery of scripture is yet to be fully opened.

Chapter Ten

RIGHTEOUS NON-INTERVENTION

Sadly, many of us can fall into a false complacency because we have sincerely convinced ourselves that we have a *sufficient understanding* of God's Plan of Salvation and have made a *sufficient effort* to be pleasing to God. We may think that we are *sufficiently versed* in scripture and have thus done all that is required of us. This is what Satan wants us to believe. But it is not what God tells us is "sufficient".

As we mentioned in an earlier chapter, when we read scripture and understand that the parable of the five wise and five foolish virgins clearly states that <u>*all*</u> ten virgins were faithful, *all* were waiting for the Lord and *all* fully expected to go with the Lord when He returned, we must begin to wonder *why* the five foolish were left behind. Why was it so important that their lamps be completely <u>*full*</u> of oil? Why is God so adamant about what is required of us?

This parable tells us that the difference between the ten virgins was that five of them had lamps which were only half filled with oil. In scripture "oil" often represents "knowledge" so this parable tells us that five of these virgins had not acquired what God wanted for the Bride of His Son. Therefore, the five foolish virgins were required to leave the place where they were waiting for the Lord so they could obtain more oil for their lamps. When they returned, with lamps filled to the brim….it was too late…the Lord had left with the five wise virgins, the door had closed to the five foolish virgins, *and they found themselves left behind.*

I repeat the lessons of this parable because we must learn the importance of **constantly** filling our hearts and minds with the word of God to such an extent that we are always **completely** filled with it. Further supporting the words and meaning of this parable is that scripture tells us that **many** will not be taken when Christ returns because of a *"lack of knowledge"* and because God says: *"I know ye not".* (Hosea 4:6) This verse in Hosea combined with the verses we read in the parable of the wise and foolish virgins are a warning to us. These verses tell us that we must increase our knowledge of scripture so we can learn what is required to truly worship God and fulfill those statutes He requires and thus ***satisfy the rules of righteousness under which God labors.***

When the Bible speaks about oil it is referencing the light we need to help us stay on track and find our way. Thus, we must replenish the oil through which we gather God's words so that the path He wishes us to take remains well lit, well defined. The oil may also represent a cleansing action where our hearts are cleansed of all guile including that which gives us a false sense of security. Many can put on a sweet and happy face while secretly harbouring a great venomous attitude toward someone. While man may not "discern" this spirit, God can.

It is therefore important to ask ourselves if we fully "know" God; know what He plans, what He offers, and what pre-requisites there may be for us to obtain the forgiveness of our sin *worthily*? Do we feel that we are so in love with our Heavenly Father and the Bridegroom of our soul that we **constantly** seek to learn of Them, **continuously** seek what They tell us through scripture, **desire** to please Them, and thus try everyday to replenish the fragrant oil of Their instruction?

Another and similar reference in scripture relating to who will be taken at the first resurrection and who will be left behind is found in Matthew 24:36-42 which tells us: *"But of that day and hour no one knows, not even the angels of heaven, but My Father only. But as the days of Noah were, so also will the coming of the Son of Man be. For as in the days before the flood, they were eating and drinking, marrying and giving in marriage, until the day that Noah entered the ark, and did not know until the flood came and took them all away, so also will the coming of the Son of Man be. Then two men will be in the field: one will be taken and the other left. Two women will be grinding at the mill: one will be taken and the other left. Watch therefore, for you do not know what hour your Lord is coming"*

And in Luke 17:36 we can read: *"Two men shall be in the field; the one shall be taken, and the other left."* But why does God seemingly choose one over another when they have obviously been co-workers or perhaps spouses of one another, and therefore perhaps practicing similar values?

If we try to understand what the "righteousness" of God really means we can unravel some of the mysteries of these requirements and learn how we must work every day to keep our "passports" to heaven up-to-date. We do not want to be left behind for "lack of knowledge". Rather we want to fully understand what God seeks in the Bride He will choose for His Son.

What then is required to help us grow and become all God longs for us to be? We want to have everything we need when it is time for us to "travel". And to accomplish this goal we must know what God tells us through scripture and examine our heart for the sinful thoughts and actions which we hide from others. Perhaps this was what separated those working in the field or sleeping in the bed.

God's righteousness is fascinating to study. *All* things are possible to our Heavenly Father, the Creator of everything, the God who is omnipresent and omnipotent. Yet God placed upon ***Himself*** the single limitation of requiring Him to labor under the rule of righteousness. Therefore, God cannot simply "pass" someone who is not truly worthy to enter His new kingdom, or be part of the Bride of Christ. If He did, He would be guilty of breaking the rules Himself. Why did God place this burden upon Himself? When we begin to question why God would place **any** restrictions upon His rule, we begin to see an incredible picture of the physics of this world and of the world which God is preparing for our future.

This world is comprised of opposites which God put into place as a part of the physics which forces our universe to function *in harmony* with all its elements. If such balances had not been put into place there would be chaos in the universe. For example, instead of the laws of gravity controlling the moon's power over the ebb and flow (opposites) of our oceans, there would be no bounds for the waters. Similarly, how would love offset the horror of evil?

As we ponder these questions and recognize that the opposite of the word "righteousness" is "unrighteousness", we realize that when our Heavenly Father chose to create and bring His plan of Salvation to fruition, He *chose* to do so *only* in and through complete and absolute righteousness. He chose this route so that **_all_** evil and **_all_** hate could be removed forever from His new kingdom.

What this means to us is that no matter how "nice" we are, there are rules…absolute rules…through which God *in His righteousness* can bless us. These blessings include …among many… the forgiveness of sin, the gift of the Holy Spirit, becoming the Bride of Christ and even becoming a resident of the New Heaven and Earth. To reach this goal we must acknowledge that God is creating this new world …… for the *righteous.* We must also realize that all evil will die, and that God, bound by righteousness cannot give us a pass no matter how "nice" or "good" we are *if we do not qualify for the passport* required of everyone else!

When we read how Abraham was granted righteousness because of His obedience, and if we carefully consider the fact that we are *not* granted the forgiveness of our sins if we have not forgiven others *and* have true remorse for what we have done, we can begin to see how these "rules" are of utmost importance.   However, when we are not aware of the "rules" of Holy Communion we may be taking this sacrament unworthily.... and sadly, many may not realize this failure because of their ***"lack of knowledge"*** regarding Holy Communion. The sacrament of Holy Communion requires four actions: acknowledging our sins, having remorse for having committed a sin, striving to overcome that sin, and forgiving others.

Further, we must remember that taking Holy Communion unworthily is dangerous to our soul salvation. Not meeting the four requirements listed aboe...before we take Holy Communion.... can bring a curse into our lives. In the following verse we can read that taking Holy Communion unworthily makes one guilty of causing the death of

Christ. 1 Corinthians 11:27 warns: "Wherefore **whosoever shall eat this bread, and drink this cup of the Lord, unworthily, shall be guilty of the body and blood of the Lord.**

When God decided to ban *all* unrighteousness, *all* evil, *all* hate, from entering the new world He is creating, God *cannot* simply display a soft heart and let us slide. He *cannot* justify allowing *any* unrighteousness to enter His new kingdom. It is not that God does not want *all* men to be saved, or that He will not forgive our sins, but what it does mean is that we take a terrible risk if we continue to bask in complacency, and we *must* watch for where we fall short. We must internalize the fact that despite God's long suffering and forbearance and His gentle heart, He has **_chosen_** to be **bound** by the rule of righteousness. Thus, we may be banned from God's new kingdom.

Again, I repeat that we can learn so much from the five virgins who were left behind who did not understand (for lack of knowledge) that they

would be left behind. They *believed* that they were ready, they *wanted* to go and were waiting to go...and they had lived their *life* to go, yet because of the *absolute* of the rules under which God chooses to operate to ban evil for all eternity, He *had* to leave the five foolish virgins behind. It was too late for them to obtain what they *then* recognized they required.

We do not want to be left behind and therefore must ask God to help us recognize where we still fall short and what we can do to be all that He longs for us to be. *Every child of God should consider what the rules of God's righteousness might mean to them.* Few understand that in God's eyes the act of talking negatively about someone is similar to murdering them. God tells us in 2 Timothy 2: 16-17 that gossip is evil; that we should not take part in it. *To God, gossip is committing murder with the tongue.* Further, Matthew 7:1 warns: *"Do not judge, or you too will be judged."*

It is not only participating in the sacrament of Holy Communion which will allow us to be a part of the First Resurrection, but it is also obtaining the knowledge we still require to please God and the commitment we need to make if we hope to become the perfect and righteous Bride.

If we consider the rules of righteousness under which God has chosen to labor *for the good of the new world He will create,* we must not as Hosea 4:6 warns, fall short for "lack of knowledge". We need to understand what God's righteousness may demand of us and look into our lives to find those things which we may be justifying as righteous "enough", but may actually cause us to become one of the five foolish virgins. Further, many have questioned God's lack of intervention where evil abounds. When some atrocities were unveiled from the past, some became convinced that God was dead; others that God had abandoned mankind. Some thought that God's lack of intervention means that He has turned His back on mankind. Some feel that what appears to be a lack of intervention does not fit the concept of a "loving, caring" God who is concerned about mankind. Many have questioned why children are abused or even murdered when God could so easily intervene but does not. One can also ask why does it appear that God does indeed intervene in some cases but not in others?

We don't yet understand what criteria exists for God or His angels to intervene and still remain in total righteousness, but we do know that God does not want Satan to have the right to say that man believes in God only because of the help God provides for them. God, to fight and destroy evil has, because of the righteousness under which He chooses to operate, **purposely** *allows evil situations to exist.*

God has even allowed evil to thrive for a period of time to prove man's faith in His plan; to demonstrate to Satan that men *choose* to follow God because they love Him and hate sin….and do so with their own free will.

Many have been shocked to read in scripture that God acknowledged Job to be a good and righteous man but nevertheless invited Satan to test him in the most terrible manner. It is a very fair question to ask why God would do this to Job.

First, it is important to note that our eternal life is forever while our life here on earth is really just a fleeting moment in time. What we suffer here will not be remembered in eternity and if it were, all of us would choose to go through it again for the perfection of what we will have. Thus, as we read the book of Job more closely and look for what God wished to accomplish, we begin to see a pattern of behavior in Job. Throughout his ordeal, Job NEVER blames God. He NEVER accuses God of being unfair. He respects God's power and RIGHT to do to him whatever He wants. He learns through his suffering that he ALWAYS will be loyal to God, trust God with his life, and LOVE God despite those terrible things God ALLOWS to happen to him. This is an amazing revelation as most of us would rail at God, would question why we were attacked and moreso question why God allowed it.

Job's loyalty to God is therefore a rather unique phenomenon and because *his loyalty could NOT be broken* by Satan's attacks, Satan finally had to sneak away from Job with his tail between his legs, defeated in his goal to break Job's faith!

Few of us have the complete dedication shown by Job toward his Heavenly Father. Few of us have such a self-less love and trust that we would ACCEPT without complaint what was happening to us. Thus the Book of Job is a true learning experience for all of us. Job lost his wife, his children, his home, his business, his friends.... and even his health. Thus Job suffered greatly at the hands of Satan **and *with God's permission* to hurt him!!!** Job even mentions that he is aware that God has allowed Satan to *"break him, take him by his neck, shake him"* (Job 16:12) and still Job does not display any anger toward God. How many of us would or could react in this manner?

But because of Job's *true* faith in God his reaction to his pain and suffering was to say: *"....naked came I out of my mother's womb, and naked shall I return thither; the Lord gave, and the Lord hath taken away;* ***blessed be the name of the Lord****."* (Job 1:21) This truly demonstrates the unblemished character within Job and what God would be so pleased to see in us.

It is clear that God wants us to help one another, teach one another, forgive one another and even rebuke one another if necessary so hand in hand we can all be found worthy of the wonder of goodness we find in scripture and meet the potential God sees in us. Further, we must never give up hope. We can always be forgiven no matter how many times we fail IF we come to our Heavenly Father in contrition, truly desiring not to commit those sins again and feeling a deep sadness in our hearts for having disappointed the God we so love. God sees into the heart. He knows when we are truthful. He knows when we "fake" it to impress others and He *deals harshly with those who present a deceitful heart to Him.*

Thus we must not be afraid to speak to God in an honest and open manner and tell Him that we truly desire to please Him. We want to become a part of the Bride of Christ and can be comforted to know that God knows our weakness…even our inherited sin which can be so difficult to overcome.

God hears our prayers, but is turned away by prayers said only to impress our audience. God sees into our heart and recognizes deceit and dishonesty. One of the many very beautiful promises God gives us in scripture are the words found in 1 Kings 9:3 which tell us: *"And the Lord said unto him, I have heard thy prayer and thy supplication, that thou hast made before me: I have hallowed this house, which thou has built, to put my name there forever; and mine eyes and mine heart shall be there perpetually."* How wonderful to have such a blessing!

When we feel that God should and does not intervene we must recall, even recite those many times we had an experience of faith and instinctively knew that God was with us, was directing our path. This works, as mentioned in the first chapter of this book, to re-train the amygdala of our brain to trust God rather than be overcome by the fears we might face in this world.

For all of us, God has already intervened. But sadly for many they chalk these experiences up to "coincidence" rather than acknowledge them as being something which the Lord did for them....to help them. When God appears not to intervene and we think he should intervene, we need to trust Him and trust that He is still in complete control of all things.....good and bad.... and will bring a blessing forth from every experience.

Proverbs 3:5 tells us: *Trust in the LORD with all thine heart; and lean not unto thine own understanding.*

Psalm 32:10 tells us: *"Many sorrows shall be to the wicked: but he that trusteth in the LORD, mercy shall compass him about."*

We may not yet understand when God does not stop evil, but when we have experienced God in our heart, we still trust that His decisions are and will be perfect.

HELEN GLOWACKI

Chapter Eleven

ANGER, END TIMES & EVIL

A true child of God strives to love, to be kind and gracious, to be long suffering and forgiving. They believe that God is in control of everything...this earth, this universe... and our lives. They understand that God is actively fulfilling His Plan of Salvation for mankind for their long term and eternal benefit, as He separates good from evil for all eternity. Therefore, it is heartbreaking for the Christian heart to be bombarded with the news that Christians all over the world are being persecuted and viciously attacked and murdered with heartless abandon. It is also shocking that these atrocities are being perpetrated without any consequences for such hateful and unjust acts.

From this heartbreaking news, we cannot help but recognize the evidence that the end time prophecies of Christian persecutions are being fulfilled. While it is difficult for the Christian mind to accept that other human beings can be so ruthless and so blind to the evil they do we can be joyful that soon Christ will come for His Bride.

While we recognize that a soul so filled with hate and ruthlessness has a demonic invasion it is still difficult to believe that a fellow human being can commit such horrendous atrocities. It is so far beyond the comprehension of the Christians gentle "heart of love" that it takes a while for us to believe that such cruelty is real; that this is here; now; and will ultimately affect every one of us.

The Bible however is our source of strength; the reason we can endure. The Bible is God's word for us, meant to teach, to provide hope, and to give us the strength we need to live through what is termed "The End Times." As we read the Bible, we learn that in general, scripture notes in *many* books of the Bible, and sometime quite *often* in a single chapter, the sequence of events in God's Plan of Salvation.

Therefore, when events are described in many chapters in the Bible, it tells us that not much time elapses between these events. This is most evident in the Book of Revelation, especially Chapters 18 through 20.

For example, Scripture tells us in Revelation 18:23-24: *"And the light of a candle shall shine no more at all in thee; and the voice of the bridegroom and of the bride shall be heard no more at all in thee......and in her was found the blood of prophets, and of saints, and of all that were slain upon the earth."*

This explains that the voices of Christians are like a candle shining through the darkness of sin and corruption. It tells us that this candle will no longer shine (to enlighten) here on earth once Christ returns and takes God's faithful to the wedding feast in heaven. But it also tells us that this candle will *shine no more* because many of those who carry the candle of godly enlightenment will be slain. Their death, and those taken at the First Resurrection, and thus removed from the earth, means that all goodness is gone, and evil will gain in strength. Grace will no longer be available. Those therefore who are left behind will be in great peril and will suffer greatly while those taken will return to Heaven with Christ for what scripture calls "The Wedding Feast" which will last for three and one half years. When this time passes, Christ and the Bride will return to earth to reign for the period of time called "The Thousand Years of Peace" or "The Millenium". All people will bow to Christ at that time.

Scripture says in Revelation 18:2: *".........Babylon ....is become the habitation of devils, and the hold of every foul spirit, a cage for every unclean and hateful bird".* And in verse 4: *"Come out of her, my people, that ye not be partakers of her sins, and that ye receive not of her plagues."* Babylon in the days of old was known as a city of sinners, thus the use of its name in this manner.

What these verses describe is that just before the coming of Christ, the blood of the saints will be shed and the devils and **foul spirits of Satan will commit terrible iniquities upon the children of God.** These verses clearly point to what is happening again today with the persecution and murder of Christians. However, God, in His loving kindness does not want us to fear these things, but to recognize what our reward will be in the end.... if we have taken God's warning to heart. Therefore, shortly following these verses, we are told in Revelation 19:7; *"Let us be glad and rejoice,* *and give honour to him, for the marriage of the Lamb **is come**; and his wife hath made herself ready."* This tells us that the dignity, and honour, and faithfulness of God's children will be rewarded, and that what they go through will not be in vain. Those called to be the Bride of Christ will see God's promise fulfilled as they enter the wedding feast where the lamb (Christ) will marry the Bride and they will become the family of God!

In Revelation 20:2-3 we are told: *"And he laid hold on the dragon, that old serpent, which is the Devil, and Satan, and bound him a thousand years. And cast him into the bottomless pit".*

And in the next verse, in Revelation 20:4 we are told: *"....and I saw the souls of them that were beheaded for the witness of Jesus, and for the word of God, and which had not worshipped the beast, neither his image, neither has received his mark upon their foreheads or in their hands; and they lived and reigned with Christ...... "*

Thus, quickly... just one chapter further, (a few verses actually)..... we are provided with the assurance that God's plan _**will**_ be fulfilled; that the faithful **will** be rewarded; and that the evil we experience **will** be stopped. Then, in Revelation, Chapter 21 and 22 we are brought to the end of the Bible where God describes the wonders of His new kingdom; the new heaven and earth He will create for the faithful. God tells us that there will be no more sorrow and no more tears....and no more fear.... for evil will never be allowed to enter God's Holy places which He plans to create for us!

But these are words which we will _**have to work**_ to believe in the face of the hate and anger we will witness. These are _words upon which our faith may falter_ as the horrors of the final battle between good and evil begins in a blatantly noticeable manner.

However, Revelation 22:12 assures us: _"And behold, I come quickly; and my reward is with me, to give every man according to his work shall be."_

And verse 17: *"And the Spirit and the bride say, Come"*. Thus whether we pray for our fellow Christians who are persecuted, or we are those who are persecuted, we must testify to and believe that God's plan is being fulfilled, that God is by our side no matter what we go through, and that if Daniel entered the lion's den and David faced Goliath, and Shadrach, Meshach and Abednego came out a fiery furnace unscathed, so will we if we can remain faithful to the end.

However, we may ***not*** stay faithful; we may falter and lose our faith. We may wonder where God is as we once again realize that evil wields so much power. We may question our faith when the unfolding of God's Plan may not come as we believed it would come. This is why God tells us not to fear and to be sure that we do not lack an understanding of His Plan of Salvation.

The answer to our lack of faith might be found in 1 Corinthians 13:11 which says: *"When I was a child,*

I spake as a child, I understood as a child, I thought as a child, but when I became a man, I put away childish things."

This important verse reminds us that life does not always go as we think it should go. That sometimes we are faced with unpleasant situations; even with horrific situations which can break our faith. Despite what we see and hear and feel......we must still go on. This verse tells us that it is time to grow up and make the decision either to trust God *__completely__* or not and teaches us that this can only be done through an understanding of God's Plan and what must occur before His plan can be completed. *__It is all about the demise of evil for all eternity!__*

We must learn to trust and we must learn not to react to hate and anger and fear. Instead we are asked to love, to understand, to have compassion, to forgive even while standing up for what is right.

In fact, reading the information we have gleaned from the previous chapters, we must, even during these terrible sufferings, act according to the tenets God has placed in our soul when we gave our word to follow Him. *We cannot hate **even when that hate is deserved.*** We cannot exact vengeance on our enemies even if we have the opportunity to do so for God tells us that vengeance is His.

Hate and anger are two different emotions. Hate is wrong and produces evil, while anger can be justified. For example, scripture tells us about God's righteous anger against those who sinned so profoundly that it caused Him to send the flood and then also to destroy the cities of Sodom and Gomorrah. Scripture tells us of Christ's anger when He overturned the tables in the marketplace outside the temple. Our own anger against injustice and evil is therefore understandable as long as we do not allow that anger to become hate.

Thus we know that God wants us to be angry about sin and evil but does not want us to exact our own vengeance. In fact, in many parts of scripture God shows us that **we cannot know what really lives in the heart of man and can easily judge someone *improperly*** and therefore tells us that we must leave all judgment to Him.

But God does teach us how to arm ourselves against the hatred and evil of the end times. He tells us in Ephesians 6:11 to: *"Put on the whole armour of God, that ye may be able to stand against the wiles of the devil."* Those "wiles" do not only encompass hatred, and evil deeds, but also the doubt and complacency which Satan can cause to grow in our hearts as we watch evil succeed. In fact, scripture clearly tell us that those who are left behind will suffer so much they will ask to die.

The "armour" of which God speaks is the power of prayer, a working knowledge of scripture and an understanding of God's Plan of Salvation. It also includes receiving the grace which God so freely offers through Holy Communion made available through the sacrifice of Christ. God tells us that as we battle evil, our shield is our **faith,** our belt is **truth**, our breastplate is **righteousness**, our boots are the **gospel**, our helmet is **salvation** and our sword is the **Holy Spirit** and **the word of God** from which come our prayers. This armour protects us from an assault by Satan and his fallen angels and since we ourselves may be weak when faced with a battle, this "armour" is what props us up to "stand against the wiles of the devil". (Ephesians 6:11-20)

Nevertheless, evil will rise more predominantly than ever before Christ returns for His Bride. The world and all its people will suffer more than ever before. **This horror will last for three and one half years** and then Christ will return with the faithful souls He'd taken at the First Resurrection and begin the reign of peace which will last for a thousand years.

When those who still remain on earth and those who already reside in eternity see Christ return, and take so many people off the earth, and then return to end the horrors, every knee will bow to Christ....*every* soul will turn to God.

Those thousand years will produce the fruits of God's love in every willing heart because during this time all evil will be bound and chained into the Lake of Fire. Mankind will thrive and know what it is to live without sin and without evil. There will be no temptation to sin.

God tells us in Revelation 21:7: *"He that overcometh shall inherit all things; and I will be his God, and he shall be my son.........But the fearful and unbelievers, and the abominable.....shall have their part in the lake which burneth....."* And in verse 27: *"And there shall in no wise enter into it anything that defileth, neither whatsoever worketh abomination, or maketh a lie, but they which are written in the Lamb's book of life."*

And in Revelation 22:2 we learn: *"...in the midst of the street....was there the tree of life which bare twelve manner of fruit....every month...."* And in verse 5 we read: *And there shall be no night there....and no need of candle, neither light of the sun, for the Lord God giveth them the light: and they shall reign forever and ever."*

Revelation 22:12 tells us*: "And behold, I come quickly, and my reward is with me. To give every man according as his work shall be."*

These are verses of encouragement so we do not grow weary of the battle but remain strong in the promises of God. God will bring our reward with Him when He returns for us!

Chapter Twelve

THE BEGINNING AND THE END

We and our religious community have quite literally boxed God into what we want to believe about him. We don't want our concepts challenged even if they are wrong or if they have limited our growth and blocked a complete understanding of the immensity and complexity of God's Plan of Salvation.

We have *expected* that the Theory of Creation does not mix with the Theory of Evolution....yet scripture shows us that they do when it points out that the Sun and Moon were not created until the end of the fourth day giving us time as we know it. We do not study the fact that the earlier days of the creation, before the sun and moon were created could have been the billions of years in which evolution thrived.

We have *expected* God's angels to look either like cherubic babies, or beautiful, gentle soft spoken white winged women in long white gowns, or even strong well-built warriors fighting Evil. We have not considered that they could instead look like double wheels with a myriad of eyes assigned to carrying a chariot. Nor do we consider that they could look like the aliens described as having no hair and standing 4 and ½ feet tall or that they could actually look like the angels described in scripture as having four faces on one head and six wings and be beautiful in God's eyes. Even though we have learned that God's "garden" was created with an incredible amount of diversity, we do not try to imagine the angel world as being similarly diverse or of us having to change our way of thinking.

We have *expected* God to intervene to prevent the atrocities of war and other evil deeds which we or our loved ones have endured. We rail at God for allowing evil the time and power in which to break our faith and lure us away from God. In fact we have even *demanded* that God intervene and when He does not, we use that as an excuse not to believe, not to follow, not to trust, not to learn and thus not even try to develop the faith God desires.

We have *expected* that God would clear the path to heaven for us. That He would remove all large obstacles and help us at every turn and overlook our complacency. But sometimes God wants to see us *working* to learn, *working* to fulfill His will, *working* to overcome our baser Adam-like nature to become more like Christ. And when we don't; when we feel it is simply too difficult or can be put off until tomorrow, we disappoint God and put our future in great jeopardy.

Nevertheless, despite our failures, God helps us. The mysteries of scripture clearly show us that God *wants* to open our understanding and shows us these mysteries as our souls are made ready to receive such special information. But in so many cases we are not ready to increase our knowledge. And sadly, for some, the hardness of their hearts cannot be bridged. Their complacency cannot be challenged.

As an example, 2 Kings 2:11 describes the time when Elijah was taken to heaven in a fiery chariot. Psalm 68:17 tells us, *"The chariots of God are twenty thousand, even thousands of angels."* And Ezekiel 10:5, 20 tells us that *"The wheels of God's chariots are Cherubim."* These verses further clarify **our current inability to open our horizons** to what God's powers really are and what He requires of us. We know from scripture what God expects of mankind as he grows in faith and begins to understand the plans God has for him. The commitment to change, to learn is dependent upon our free will to *want* to learn and change.

Acts 17:16 tells us that everyone worships something and thus many worship the idols of money, fame, lust, power, self, hate and even sports! These must all be laid aside if we worship God in His Trinity of Father, Son and Holy Spirit and work to overcome the idolatry which tempts us every day. To do so, we must first acknowledge the danger of our idols.

Acts 17:24 tells us that *"God that made the world and all things therein, seeing that He is Lord of heaven and earth. dwelleth not in temples made with hands."* And in verse 31: *"Because he hath appointed a day, in the which he will judge the world in righteousness by that man whom he hath ordained; whereof he hath given assurance unto all men, in that he hath raised him from the dead."*

As we look at scripture we find many references to God being in control *of the entire Universe…*of the stars and the heavens, the weather and the minutest occurrences here on earth. Interestingly, even great minds such as physicist Paul C. Davies states: *"…to* *be a scientist, you had to have faith that the universe is governed by dependable, immutable, absolute, universal, mathematical laws of an unspecified origin. You've got to believe that these laws won't fail, that we won't wake up tomorrow to find heat flowing from cold to hot, or the speed of light changing by the hour. Over the years I have often asked my physicist colleagues why the laws of physics are what they are? ...The favorite reply is, 'There is no reason they are what they are--they just are.*

Even over time, scientists have noted that these laws of nature remain consistent. The same laws which we find on earth also govern a star billions of light years away. A recent study stated: *"One of the most important numbers in physics, the proton-electron mass ratio, is the same in a galaxy six billion light years away as it is here on Earth, according to new research, laying to rest debate about whether the laws of nature vary in different places in the Universe."*

All of modern science rests in the belief that rational laws exist in the universe. The main category of modern scientists who propelled exploration and discovery of these laws were men and women who believed in the existence of an all-powerful God. This is because they envisioned the universe to follow laws in keeping with the rationality and majesty of God. Just as God is consistent and unchanging, there is a constant and unchanging nature of science. These scientists believe that God made the universe to operate lawfully, according to divine reason and with glorious beauty. Even the famous scientist Albert Einstein said: *"God does not play with dice"!*

This is quite different from people who believed in multiple gods, each affecting the universe by their own whim, temperament or talent. In polytheistic societies, the gods were inconsistent and unsearchable and nature was, according to their beliefs, governed by gods who could not be known. They believed that the universe behaved in as much of a mystery as their gods, with little thought that it could be otherwise. The concept of a discoverable, intelligent, orderly universe which is rational and predictable simply was not in their worldview.

However, followers of Christ believe God to be rational, wise and *willing to be known by* showing Himself through Christ. Throughout the Bible are statements such as found in Romans 1:19-21: *"For what can be known about God is plain to them (people), because God has shown it to them. For his invisible attributes, namely, his eternal power and divine nature, have been clearly perceived, ever since the creation of the world, in the things that have been made."*

Modern science's greatest advancements came from people who believed what the scriptures say in John 1:33 and Colossians1:16: *"All things were created through Him and for Him. And He is before all things, and in Him all things hold together."*

They believed that God created **everything** and ordered it in a rational way, for humankind's discovery, benefit, and growth, *and for God's glory* so mankind would recognize God's power and majesty. Sir Isaac Newton and his contemporaries believed that in performing scientific experiments, they were uncovering the divine plan for the universe in the form of its underlying mathematical order.

Some leading scientists whose work was motivated by their faith were: Copernicus, Kepler, Galileo, Brahe, Descartes, Boyle, Newton, Leibniz, Gassendi, Pascal, Mersenne, Cuvier, Harvey, Dalton, Faraday, Herschel, Joule, Lyell, Lavoisier, Priestley, Kelvin, Ohm, Ampere, Steno, Pasteur, Maxwell, Planck, Mendel.

These scientists were convinced that God created a magnificent *universe* which could be mathematically measured, leading to precise and valuable discoveries. This led to such discoveries as Kepler's third law stating that the square of the time of a planet's revolution is proportional to the cube of its mean distance from the sun. Kepler came to this conclusion because he was convinced that there had to be a beautiful mathematical relationship which was hidden and waiting to be discovered. He felt that this was put in place by an orderly God whose intellect is far beyond ours.

Michao Kaku, one of today's well respected scientists, pioneered the "String Theory" of the universe which deems that the universe is formed by *many* dimensions of space and time. This theory supports what we have discussed earlier regarding the amazing capabilities of UFO's and God's angels.

Biblical scholars are convinced that hidden in scripture and awaiting man's discoveries therein is mention of how those beings from other parts of the universe have come to earth for a specific reason. It is for us to learn whether or not these beings (whether angelic or not) came to earth to further educate mankind such as is believed about ancient civilizations, or to gather information about the progress of mankind and their readiness for the return of Christ. Nevertheless, they believe that everything is known by and initiated by God.

What this means to us is that we must begin to "know" God far better than we do now. We must look **outside and beyond** the range of where we have so far kept God. We must open our minds and hearts to the fact that God is far more than we'd previously understood. But we must also learn what He asks of us so we can obtain the "passport" necessary to being a part of His new Heaven and Earth.

Most of us (and our religious communities) have kept God and His plan for mankind in a little box which we can manage and justify. But now may be the time for us to expand that thinking and acknowledge that God, His universe, the heavens he governs, and the angels who do His bidding are so much greater than we have realized.

Psalm 8:4-6 asks the question: *"What is man that thou art mindful of him, or the son of man, that thou carest for him? Thou didst make him [man] for a little while lower than the angels, thou hast crowned him with glory and honor, putting everything in subjection under his [man's] feet."*

God left nothing on earth outside the control of man *IF* he had the faith of one grain of a mustard seed. As it is, we do not yet see everything in subjection to man because of our lack of faith, lack of understanding and sinful nature.

Hebrews 2:9-11 tells us: *"Jesus, who for a little while was made lower than the angels, was crowned with glory and honor because of the suffering of death, so that by the grace of God he might taste death for everyone. For it was fitting that he, for whom and by whom all things exist, in bringing many sons to glory, should make the pioneer of their salvation perfect through suffering. For he who makes whole and those who are made whole have all one body. That is why he is not ashamed to call them brethren, saying, "I will proclaim thy name to my brethren, in the midst of the congregation I will praise thee." And again, "I will put my trust in him." And again, "Here am I, and the children God has given me. Since therefore the children share in flesh and blood, he himself likewise partook of the same nature, that through death he might destroy him who has the power of death, that is, the devil, and deliver all those who through fear of death were subject to lifelong bondage.*(Hebrews 2:6-15)

A short cryptic verse immediately precedes this description of the restorative work of Jesus: **"For it was not to angels that God subjected the world to come, of which we are speaking."**(Heb. 2:5) As we consider this statement we begin to recognize that the Thousand Year Kingdom of Peace or the Millennial kingdom which immediately follows the return of Christ is **not** governed by the angels, yet angels <u>do</u> have a prominent role in how God governs the present age.

Even the book of Job begins with a description of the *bene elohim*, (angels), appearing in heaven before the throne of God. Among them is Satan. In order to help Job recognize his own deeper character, God allows Satan to test Job to the limits. God's one pre-requisite is that Job's life is to be spared:

And the LORD said to Satan, *"Behold, all that Job has is in your power; only upon himself do not put forth your hand." So Satan went forth from the presence of the LORD. Now there was a day when his sons and daughters were eating and drinking wine in their eldest brother's house; and there came a messenger to Job, and said, "The oxen were plowing and the asses feeding beside them; and the Sabeans fell upon them and took them, and slew the servants with the edge of the sword; and I alone have escaped to tell you." While he was yet speaking, there came another, and said, "The fire of God fell from heaven and burned up the sheep and the servants, and consumed them; and I alone have escaped to tell you." While he was yet speaking, there came another, and said, "The Chaldeans formed three companies, and made a raid upon the camels and took them, and slew the servants with the edge of the sword; and I alone have escaped to tell you." While he was yet speaking, there came another, and said, "Your sons and daughters were eating and drinking wine in their eldest brother's house; and behold, a great wind came across the wilderness, and struck the four corners of the house, and it fell upon the young people, and they are dead; and I alone have escaped to tell you..." Again there was a day when the sons of God came to present themselves before the LORD, and Satan also came among them to present himself before the LORD. And the LORD said to Satan, "Whence have you come?" Satan answered the LORD, "From going to and fro on the earth, and from walking up and down on it." And the LORD said to Satan, "Have you considered my servant Job, that there is none like him on the earth, a blameless and upright man, who fears God and turns away from evil? He still holds fast his integrity, although you moved me against him, to destroy him without cause."* **Then Satan answered the LORD,** *"Skin for skin! All that* *a man has he will give for his life. But put forth thy hand now, and touch his bone and his flesh, and he will curse thee to thy face."* **And the LORD said to Satan,** *"Behold, he is in your power; only spare his life." So Satan went forth from the presence of the LORD, and afflicted Job with loathsome sores from the sole of his foot to the crown of his head. And he took a potsherd with which to scrape himself, and sat among the ashes.* (Job 1:12-2:8)

Much sound theology is found in this passage: As mentioned in a previous chapter, Satan can do nothing without permission from the Lord and must always stay within appointed bounds. Yet he apparently has been given power over raiding bands of nomads, over weather, and the forces of nature, and over Job's physical health.

This passage does not imply that Satan causes *all* disease and suffering, or that *all* natural disasters are Satan's mischief. But from Job we gain the insight that when Jesus calmed the raging storm on the Sea of Galilee He may have spoken to an angel.

"One day Jesus got into a boat with his disciples, and he said to them, 'Let us go across to the other side of the lake.' So they set out, and as they sailed he fell asleep. And a storm of wind came down on the lake, and they were filling with water, and were in danger. And they went and woke him, saying, 'Master, Master, we are perishing!' And he awoke and rebuked the wind and the raging waves; and they ceased, and there was a calm. He said to them, 'Where is your faith?' And they were afraid, and they marveled, saying to one another, 'Who then is this, that he commands even wind and water, and they obey him?'" (Luke 8:22-25)

It is important to recognize that God uses "messengers," better known to us by the Greek word: "angels" in the governing and teaching of mankind. The Biblical view of the universe is not the modern one of vast reaches of barren space interrupted every couple of million miles or so by asteroids. The Biblical view of *the universe is that it is teeming and throbbing with life everywhere,* and is heavily populated with "legions" and "myriads" of angelic beings of various ranks (Colossians 1:16) and **"species"**. (see, for instance, the descriptions in Ezekiel 1:5-25 and Revelation 4:6-8).

Angels are also associated with astronomical phenomena throughout the Bible (Judges 5:20; Job 38:7; Isaiah 14:13; Matthew 24:29; Jude 13; Revelation 1:20; 8:10-12; 9:1;12:4) as well as with the activity of the weather. For instance, wind, storms, and lightning are spoken of in connection with the actions of God and the angels in both blessing and curse (Genesis 8:1; 41:27; Exodus 10:13,19; 14:21; 15:10; 19:16; Numbers 11:31; Psalm 18:10; 104:3,4; 107:25; 135:7; 147:18;148:8; Ezekiel 1:4ff; Matthew 24:31; John 3:8; Acts 2:2; Revelation 7:1-3; 8:5,7; 16:8, 17, 18). Clearly, the Biblical world view does not attribute changes in weather to *impersonal* "forces" or "processes:"

Angels are the powers of God, and they never cease working. God sustains the world through His energy, He governs everything so that not even a sparrow falls to the ground without His decree.

(Matthew 10:29)Martin Luther took the psalmist's statement very seriously believing that the wind has wings and after a violent storm, said: *"The devil provokes such storms, but good winds are produced by good angels. Winds are nothing but spirits, either good or evil. The devil sits there and snorts, and so do the angels when the winds are salubrious."*

Thus the Biblical world view is uncompromising: God is running the Universe thus every atom in the universe is under His command. His Word created and sustains Him and is why He can assert His power and authority in such absolute terms.

Isaiah 45:7I tells us that God forms the light and creates darkness further stating: *"I make peace and create calamity: I, the LORD, do all these things. Who can speak and have it happen if the Lord has not decreed it?"* And in Lamentations 3:37, 38: *Is it not from the mouth of the Most High that both calamities and good things come?*

Thus it is time for us to embrace a new era for our faith where we will no longer misunderstand and mis-state God's power over <u>everything</u>. It is time for us to learn the enormity of God's reach and creativity **throughout the entire universe and through all time and dimension**. If we can do this, God will smile and we will be blessed with a lack of fear and a joyful overwhelming love and appreciation for God.

1 Timothy 1:7 reminds us: *"For God has not given us a spirit of fear, but of power and of love and of a sound mind."* And 2 Corinthians 4:16 comforts with the words: *"Therefore we do not lose heart. Even though our outward man is perishing, yet the inward man is being renewed day by day."*

Psalm 119:18 shows us that we are to ask God *to "open my eyes that I may see"*. Praying in this manner will let God see that we desire with all our hearts, not to find ways to doubt but to find ways to open ourselves to all that God has made and desires for the future He so beautifully describes and offers to us.

We do not want to be left behind for our lack of knowledge but taken because we have never stopped trusting His plan for us. It isn't hard to please God but He does have certain requirements which we *must* fulfill to be found worthy to enter His new kingdom of righteousness.

The reward is beautifully stated in Deuteronomy 3:10: *"The LORD shall command the blessing upon thee in thy storehouses, and in all that thou settest thine hand unto; and he shall bless thee in the land which the LORD thy God giveth thee".*

Thus, I'd like to end this book with the words from Luke 12:32 which assures us: *"Fear not little flock... for it is the Father's good pleasure to give you the kingdom...."*

Helen Glowacki

HELEN GLOWACKI

OUR PRAYER:

Dear Heavenly Father: We come to Thee with a humbled heart, aware of Your power, of the immensity of Your Plan of Salvation, and of Your incredible love and concern for each of us. We also come to acknowledge our faults and failings and ask you to forgive us. Forgive also our lack of knowledge, our lack of belief and our lack of commitment to You and open our closed and hardened hearts to what You offer. Help us make the commitment which can bring us the fullness of Your blessing and a path to the First Resurrection. Please take away our lackadaisical attitude and our complacency, and let us appreciate the gift of grace and love which you extend to all of mankind. Please be with us and our loved ones, please forgive us the past and let us begin anew. Teach us what we need to know, help us to work at learning your words, trusting them and doing as You ask. Make us worthy to become a part of the Bride of Christ. Help us appreciate every day the great sacrifice the Lord Jesus made for us and the love in Your heart that caused You to plan a future for us. We thank you from the bottom of our heart for hearing our pleas and pray in the name of Your Son, the Lord Jesus. Amen.

HELEN GLOWACKI

SCRIPTURAL INDEX

ANGELS, ALIENS & CHARIOTS

ANGELS, ALIENS & CHARIOTS

ANGELS, ALIENS & CHARIOTS

Jude 13	*"...blackness of darkness forever."*	
Revelation 1:20	*"...the seven stars are the angels..."*	
Revelation 8:10-12	*"Then the third angel sounded..."*	
Revelation 9:1	*"...I saw a star fallen..."*	
Revelation 12:4	*"His tail drew a third of the stars..."*	
Genesis 8:1	*"...God made a wind..."*	
Genesis 41:27	*"...blighted by the east wind..."*	
Exodus 10:13	*"...the east wind brought the locust."*	
Exodus 10:19	*"...the Lord turned a very strong west wind..."*	
Exodus 14:21	*"...the Lord caused the sea to go back..."*	
Exodus 15:10	*"You blew with Your wind..."*	
Exodus 19:16	*"...there were thunderings and lightnings..."*	
Numbers 11:31	*"Now a wind went out..."*	
Psalm 18:10	*"...the wings of the wind..."*	
Psalm 104:3-4	*"...Who makes the clouds His chariot..."*	
Psalm 107:25	*"...His wonders in the deep..."*	
Psalm 135:7	*"...He makes lightning..."*	
Psalm 147:18	*"...the waters flow."*	
Psalm 148:8	*"Fire and hail..."*	
Ezekiel 1:4	*"...a great cloud with raging fire..."*	
Matthew 24:31	*"...the four winds..."*	
John 3:8	*"The wind blows where it wishes..."*	
Acts 2:2	*"...a rushing mighty wind..."*	
Revelation 7:1-3	*"...holding the four winds..."*	
Revelation 8:5	*"...thundering, lightnings and an earthquake..."*	
Revelation 8:7	*"...hail and fire followed..."*	
Revelation 16:8	*"...scorch men with fire."*	
Revelation 16:17	*"...his bowl into the air..."*	
Revelation 16:18	*"...a great earthquake..."*	267
Matthew 10:29	*"...not one of them falls..."*	
Isaiah 45:7	*"I make peace and create calamity..."*	
Lamentations 3:37	*"Who is he who speaks..."*	
Lamentations 3:38	*"...from the mouth of the Most High..."*	
1 Timothy 1:7	*"God has not given us the spirit of fear..."*	268
2 Corinthians 4:16	*"Therefore we do not lose heart..."*	
Psalm 119:18	*"...open my eyes..."*	
Deuteronomy 3:10	*"The Lord shall command the blessing..."*	269
Luke 12:32	*"Fear not little flock..."*	
Luke 11:11-13	*"...if a son ask for bread, how much.."*	306

HELEN GLOWACKI

BIBLIOGRAPHY

The Holy Bible, King James Version, published by The New Apostolic Church, Canada, Thomas Nelson, Inc., Camden, NJ, 1972

James Strong, LLD, STD, *Strong's Exhaustive Concordance of the Bible*, Abington, Nashville, thirty fourth printing 1996, copyright 1890

Henry H. Halley, *Halley's Bible Handbook*, Zondervan Publishing House, Grand Rapids, Michigan, 24th edition, Copyright 1965

Henry M. Morris, *Many Infallible Proofs*, Moody Press, Chicago, 3rd printing 1977

Henry M. Morris, *The Bible and Modern Science*, Moody Press, Chicago, 1951, 1968

The Apocrypha: I Esdras, II Esdras, Tobit, Ecclesiasticus

The Layers of the Ocean as portrayed on the Sea & Sky website

Donald Grey Barnhouse, *The Invisible War*, Zondervan Publishing House, Grand Rapids, Michigan, 12th printing 1976 copyright 1965

Robert Boyd, *Boyd's Bible Handbook*, Eugene, Oregon: Harvest House, 1983

The Book of Enoch translated by R.H. Charles in
1917 and found via the Internet on www.sacred
text.org

Roget's II The New Thesaurus, Houghton Mifflin
Company, Boston, 1980, by the editors of *The
American Heritage Dictionary.*

Dinesh DeSouza's observations in a debate at Tufts
University in 2008

ABOUT THE AUTHOR

Helen Glowacki is an interior designer, writer, teacher, and motivational speaker. She was the host, writer, and producer of the television series "The Contemporary Woman", broadcast by UA Columbia Cablevision. Her writing credentials include an extensive background as a freelance feature and staff writer for four newspapers and for various newsletters and magazines.

A graduate of William Paterson University, Helen received a Bachelor of Arts degree, magna cum laude, in Communications. She also received an Associate of Science degree with honors and is a registered nurse.

Helen donates her books to cancer centers, drug rehabilitation centers, and prisons. She also donates them to the mission schools of *The Henwood Foundation* to use her gift for writing to help others find the love and comforting presence of God. Helen has recently developed "Scriptural Insight, Inc." which is a charitable foundation (501C3) through which she provides her mini-books, brochures and novels and finds thosewho willhelp bring testimony to others. Helen has written a number of well received Christian articles filled with insight about scripture and how God wants us to conduct our lives. She posts many of her articles on Face Book, and on her website.

Those who have provided reviews of Helen's books tout the beautiful stories in her novels and speak of her non-fiction books as spiritually uplifting and biblically correct. Her greatest joys are her husband, children, and grandchildren, and time spent in church and in fellowship.

FOR MORE INFORMATION:

For general information: Visit the author's website at: www.helenglowacki.com

To purchase a book by Helen Glowacki: Visit her website or Amazon.com.

For information about Helen's charitable foundation: Visit www.scripturalinsight.org.

Excerpt from the Mini-Book

"WHAT DO ANGELS DO?"

This is a wonderful and incredibly informative book about angels. It describes the three levels of heaven, the three major duties of the angels, the hierarchy of the angels and the nine types of angels who inhabit these realms.

It explains why spiritual warfare exists, what powers Satan has and why evil is so strong. It also addresses what role we will play when Christ returns. Interestingly, the Seraphim, Cherubim and Thrones are described in scripture as "Counselors". The Dominions, Virtues and Powers have the duties of "Governors" and the Principalities, Archangels and Angels are the "Messengers.

This seventh book in Helen's mini-book series is 126 pages long.   ISBN: 978-0-9847211-8-4

HELEN GLOWACKI

LIST AND DESCRIPTION OF BOOKS
written by Helen Glowacki

NOVELS
(Book Size 6 x 9)

When God BrokeGrandma's Heart: (208 pages) Rising from sorrow to become a beacon of faith Grandma struggles in an abusive marriage until God moves her from unequally yoked and broken to the healing of His love and forgiveness. Her granddaughter Sarah learns where to find answers to her problems and carries that legacy to those she loves. **Paperback: ISBN 978-0-9847-2110-8**

When God Took Grandma Home: (260 pages) About the heartache of drug addiction, of the enemy who destroys children through drugs, why God allows righteous anger, why we should pray for those in eternity and a description an incredible experience of faith for Matt and Sarah about why God allowed such heartache to occur. **Paperback: ISBN 978-0-49847-2111-5**

When Grandma Chased the Spirits: (208 Pages) The magnetism of idolatry, it's invisible power, and the heartache of bearing a child out of wedlock brings debilitating panic attacks to Mary and affects her husband Kevin. When Matt and Sarah tell them about their faith, God engineers a miracle to solve what that they thought impossible to resolve. **Paperback: ISBN 978-0-9847-2112-2**

The Granddaughter and the Monkey Swing: (284 pages) A wedding, a broken engagement, renovating and decorating a home through Divine Proportion, the truth about Halloween, and the gift of role models create a tender story of friendship. Helping through the planning and problems of a wedding culminates in the unveiling of a secret. **Paperback: ISBN 978-0- 9847-2113-9**

Grandma's Little Book of Poetry: The Story of God's Plan of Salvation: (277 pages) This beautiful whimsical story for all ages, begins when Sarah finds a manuscript in Grandma's desk and recognizes the story Grandma read to her and Josh and Caleb when they were children. Angels watch the inhabitants below them struggle to find God. **Paperback: ISBN 978-0-9847-2114-6**

Abiding Faith, Hidden Treasure: (262 pages) Serving in Iraq, Jim loses his faith to see a loving God allow so much heartache. Barbara invites him to dinner where Grandma shows him why creation and evolution co-exist and God's enemy creates the injustices Jim blames on God. Letters from the grave bring an incredible experience of faith. **Paperback: ISBN 978-0-9847-2115-3**

__And Then They Asked God__: (295 Pages) WhenRebecca and Jayden arrive at their college campus they are overwhelmed by betrayal. Losing the values Rebecca once cherished fills her with guilt so monumental that she cannot forgive herself. Chaldeth the evil angel is defeated when God's grace frees Jayden and brings Rebecca's recovery. **Paperback: ISBN 978-0-9847-2116-7**

__Caleb's Testimony__: (262 pages) Caleb would have taken bets on his ability to trust God explicitly....until his accident.. Now, he and Ann must face the wrath of Satan aimed at causing them to blame God for their misfortune. **Paperback: ISBN 978-0-9847-2119-1.**

"WHY GOD WHY"MINI-SERIES
by Helen Glowacki

(Book Size 5 ½ x 8)

__To What Purpose__?: (126 pages) This first book in the *Why God Why* series answers questions about why we are here, what we need to learn, and what God plans for us. It is an excellent book for testimony and one you will share with others. **Paperback: ISBN 978-1-4507-7580-9**

__Why God, Why__?: (126 pages) This second book in the *Why God Why* Series describes why we experience heartache, its

purpose, and how to face it. It answers questions about God's plan for us and what we need to do to be found worthy.
Paperback: ISBN 978-1-4507-7581-6

Why Trust Scripture?: (126 pages) This third book in the *Why God, Why* Series addresses the challenges against scripture, who wrote the Bible, the importance of the sacraments, what role Satan plays, and how health and the Bible are related. **Paperback: ISBN 978-1-4507-7582-3**

***What Should I Know about Life after Death and the Coming Tribulation*?**: (126 pages) What occurs following death, what will happen during the tribulation, and what the seven seals could mean to us are explained in this fourth book of the series. **Paperback: ISBN 978-1-4507-7583-0**

***What Does God Want Me to do Right Now*?**: (126 pages) A concise explanation of what God asks of us, how we can live up to His expectations what is required to become a part of the Bride of Christ, and what God plans for the future with or without us. **Paperback: ISBN 978-1 4507-9076-5**

***Do The Little Sins Really Count*?** (126 pages) Most of us believe that the little sins don't really matter but scripture explains why they do. **Paperback: ISBN: 978-0-9847-2117-7**

__What Do Angels Do__? (126 pages) This seventh book in the Why God Why series explains the role of the angels created by our Heavenly Father. It describes the nine types of angels, the three heavens they occupy and the three major roles they play in our lives. **Paperback: ISBN 978-0-9847-2118-4**

__What is Faith__?(126 pages) This eighth book in the Why God Why series addresses how we obtain faith, how we can increase our faith and what can break our faith. It also addresses how God is bound by the rules of righteousness when he intervenes in people's lives. **Paperback: ISBN 978-0-9893-8076-8**

__Satan's Gift of Fear__ (126 Pages) This ninth book in the Why God Why series by Helen Glowacki explains the root of fear, why the body remembers past experiences, what we should fear, how we can overcome panic attacks, and why God worries that it is fear which can break our faith. **Paperback: ISBN 978-0-9893-8078-2**

OTHER NON-FICTION BOOKS
By Helen Glowacki

(Book Size 5 ½ x 8 ½)

__Politically Incorrect: The Get Some Gumption Handbook For When Enough is Enough__: (406 pages) Fifty timely and controversial issues are examined under the politically correct approach and compared to what scripture tells us is the approach that God wants His children to take.   **Paperback: ISBN 978-1-4507-9074-1**

Overcoming Depression: How To Be Happy:(258 pages) We all face heartache, and all feel sad from time to time. But depression lingers and can result from many different causes. It can rob us of hope and destroy our relationship with God. Thus our Heavenly Father tells us through scripture how we can tap into His blessing and His direction and brings joy out of tribulation. **Paperback: ISBN 978-1-4507-9077-2**

What No One Tells You About Addictions: (216 pages) Discussing the merits of tough love, the selfish co-dependency of the enabler, what scripture tells us about spiritual warfare and invasion, and generational sin, make this book a must read. **Paperback: ISBN 978-1- 4507--9075-8**

Angels, Aliens and Chariots: (300 pages) Why does God mention the fear we will experience during the end times over 365 times throughout scripture? Why did God create angels with four faces and others as wheels covered with eyes? Why does God's righteousness prevent Him from intervening against evil? Is there a relationship here to UFO sightings? This is a must read which opens the mind, points out the future, and shows us how to remain faithful to the end. **Paperback: ISBN 978-9780-9893-8079-9**

BOOK REVIEWS

Reverend (District Apostle Ret.) Richard C. Freund, President of The New Apostolic Church, USA, Sea Cliff, New York: Magnificent writer, a story which makes the reader become emotionally involved, a joy to read, strong Christian values. *"When God Broke Grandma's Heart",* best seller quality.

Reverend (District Apostle Ret.) Richard C. Freund, President of The New Apostolic Church, USA. Helen's new novel,*"When God Took Grandma Home"* "Delights, brings comfort to those who grieve. Inspires, gives insight into the after-life, masterful portrayal.

Reverend Andrew Muliokela: New Apostolic Church in Alexandria, Virginia, formerly from Zambia Africa:*The Granddaughter and the Monkey Swing* and this series of books are awesome! A journey unlike another, I was reading a great novel, learning about confidence, love and support but also learning Bible verses at the same time! Helen Glowacki teaches through her books and I recommend them 100%. You'll enjoy the journey!

Reverend Frederick Rothe, (Ret. New Apostolic Church, New York) Palm Beach Gardens Congregation, Florida: Spent 48 years serving God and another 30 in the congregation. These books contain an accurate account of what God wants of us and why we suffer. The application of scripture and the people in the stories stand for the principles God wants in all of us.

Reverend Kevin Speranza, New Apostolic Church, Palm Beach Gardens, Florida: *And Then They Asked God* so happy I read this, weaves, documents biblical precepts, addresses political correctness, moral & political corruption, biased teaching, insidious growth of socialism renamed progressivism, self-importance, guilt and its debilitating power. WELL DONE! Identifies danger, artfully and Biblically addresses them.

Reverend Luke Jansen, Sr. V. P., Medical Connections,Boca Raton, Florida: "To Ms. Glowacki, author of **The Grandma Series**: grateful for your books, refreshing to find a Christian author who sees the *difference* between religion and spirituality AND that the two can and should be used in the same sentence.

Reverend Derryck Beukes, Montana-De Aar Congregation, Northern Cape, South Africa: Dear Helen, I personally often use your articles in my soul care visits, especially where youth are involved. I can assure you that your articles made a difference to my way of thinking, and I am busy encouraging fellow priests to read your works, as they are so factual and insightful! Thank you for your hard work. I thank God for you, and the wisdom He gave you! Please continue with the excellent work.

Deacon Shadreck Wilima, Overspill Congregation, Ndola, Zambia: Your articles prompt realistic examples which New Apostolic Christians need for their everyday living.

Youth Chairperson, Sunday School Teacher, Mulenga Ernest, Lusaka Central Congregation, Lusaka, Zambia: Through your writing I am constantly reminded of what to be aware of. I pray that God keeps you in the hollow of His hand, guards you and guides you to reach your brethren as you do me. Thanks for caring for the souls of many.

Reverend Aurelio Cerullo, Atripalda Congregation in Campania, Southern Italy: Dear Helen, your books and articles, and social networking bring brothers and sisters the words of our faith and touch the hearts of those who do not know our faith. Our goal isfound through the grace of the apostolate and in this sense, the word's from 1 Corinthians 15:58 assumes an important meaning: *"Therefore, my beloved brethren, be steadfast, immovable, always abounding in the work of the Lord, Knowing That your labor is not in vain in* *the Lord".* Now that I am a minister of God for about a year I too am grateful to our beloved Father in Heaven for having opened the eyes of my soul, for having removed the plugs from my ears of my heart to hear and listen to His will in connection and communion with those who precede us, guided by the light of the Holy Spirit. God's work always evolves and adapts to the times and even via computers, cell phones and smart phones. I Thank God for having been able to know you, you're a very valuable pearl. God bless you richly.

Rev. Fred Krueger, (Ret.) Lutheran Minister 12 yrs and Clinical Social Worker 26 years, Dallas, Texas: "Inspiring, grabs the heart, author headed to the bestseller list, a pleasure to read, masterful. *"When God Took Grandma Home"* filled with insight into God's plan!

NOTE: The articles which are referred to in these reviews are excerpts from Helen Glowacki's non-fiction books. Not shown are reviews by the ministers who oversee *The Henwood Foundation*'s New Apostolic Mission Schools in Zambia and review all reading materials prior to distribution.

Edith Stier, wife of a Ret. District Evangelist, Clifton, New Jersey: *The Grandma Series* helps those in need, inspirational, heartwarming, ends with a beautiful example of how God explains our pain, renews hope, shows us the way, creates miracles. I love this series.

Patricia Robinson, wife of a Ret. Rector, Indiana: 5 star rating: *When God Broke Grandma's Heart*: WONDERFUL INSPIRATIONAL NOVEL, enjoyed this book, well written, Bible references, how to achieve peace of mind and soul.

Thomas Cecil, Palm Coast, Florida: *Angels, Aliens and Chariots* expanded my belief in how everything around us is so connected. I was awe inspired that the author covered so many different ideas which most of us only occasionally think about. Her knowledge of God and scripture is amazing. I was intrigued with the entire content of this book and found myself not wanting to put the book downas I was anxious to absorb everything in this book as quickly as possible.

Rosemarie Schaal, wife of an Ret. Reverend, New York:_Abiding Faith, Hidden Treasure:_ Reader develops empathy, feels emotion, hears a battle between scientific and spiritual knowledge. Skillful, detailed, brilliant, vivid, teaches that nothing happens that is not planned by Him.

Colette van Loggerenberg, wife of a Minister, Scottsville Congregation of Pietermaritzberg, South Africa: _Grandma's Little Book of Poetry: The Story of God's Plan of Salvation:_ This has to be one of the BEST EVER books that I have read....If you ever get the chance to get one of Helen's novels...READ IT. It's like a fairytale but a TRUE fairytale.....Close your eyes and picture this: Grandma with her hair in a bun, glasses perched delicately on her nose, sitting in a rocking chair and her grandchildren sitting on the floor with BIG eyes hanging onto her every word.....but with a twist!!!!! If you have doubts about PRAYER...read this book. I LOVED IT...thank you!

Debbie Espeland, wife of a Rector, Palm Beach Gardens Congregation, Florida: 5 star rating: _When God Took Grandma Home:_ HEARTWARMING! This book touched my heart. It is both heartwarming and very spiritual.

Aletta Venter, wife of a Deacon, Scottsville Congregation, Pietermaritzburg, South Africa: _"Grandma's Little Book of Poetry: The Story of God's Plan of Salvation"._ What a learning process for me. Oooh I just **love** the way the angels are telling the story, **very original!** When is mankind ever going to learn? The inhabitant's lesson was to learn of good and evil. And they failed miserably each time. The devil has his agenda, and the inhabitants are the target. They call upon God for help, the angels rejoiced. Great....!!!

Aletta Venter, wife of a Deacon, Pietermaritzburg, South Africa: _"Abiding Faith, Hidden Treasure"_ is the deepest and most rewarding novel I have ever read, touched my soul, made me cry, author's understanding of God's work is astounding, opens the mysteries

Lisa Mayo, wife of Minister, Palm Beach Gardens Congregation, Florida: Helen's *Why God Why* series of books gave me a new understanding of my faith. They are informative, so enlightening and in-depth, but in a way that is easily understood!!

Tammera Shelton, M.S. Psychology, Odenton, Maryland: I find *"When God Broke Grandma's Heart"* inspirational, beautifully portrays need to let go of negative events and that despite injustice, no pain is for naught.

Robert W. Rothe, USMC 1970-1976, Nevada: 5 star rating: *When God Broke Grandma's Heart:* Outstanding writer, kept me riveted, an angel sent to help through trying days. Thank you for helping me find peace.

Katharina Leipp, Schopfheim, Germany: This is the first time I have ever heard of a female New Apostolic author and I am very impressed by your articles. I have sent your link to my Shepherd and German friends and would like you to consider advertising in our German *Our Family Magazine.*

Theresa Cecil, Palm Coast, Florida: *Angels, Aliens and Chariots* gives the reader insight into the meaning of God's love and plan of salvation for mankind. The author uses scripture to provide examples of God's words since the beginning of Creation, through to ancient civilizations to our current "End Times" and even explains why things in the past had to unfold as they did..

Claudine Visagie, South Africa: I'm trying to think of a way to introduce Helen's books and articles to others… especially to our youth. They are life changing!

Rabecca Mukuta Mukato, Lusaka, Zambia, Africa: Speaking on behalf of my Dad, District Elder Mukato, your articles are brilliant because they have changed me! Because of your articles my Dad has less headaches!

Robert Henry Parkes, Pietermaritzburg, South Africa: You are gifted with the verses and writings you do and are so inspiring to others. God is really using you as His special servant. You are really a wonderful person and we thank the Lord for you our sister in faith.

Frank Geores, from Port St. Lucie, Florida: *"When Grandma Chased The Spirits:* beautiful spiritual experience, can see caring nature and loving heart of author, eloquently reveals her love for God and search for truth. Worthy of the Star of Bethlehem rating. Thank you for sharing your magnificent gift.

Ben Lodwick, Avid Reader., from Brookfield, Wisconsin: Wow! An eye opener about God's plan of salvation, and why bad things happen to good people. Reminds me of Jim LaHaye and Jerry B. Jenkins "Left Behind Series". MUST READ!"

Dr. Walter Forman From North Palm Beach, Florida:*Grandma's Little Book of Poetry: The Story of God's Plan of Salvation:* a "wonderful book about success and failure in life. All Helen's novels are wonderful, a balm for the soul and an education to the seeker."

Ed Ruiter from Ontario, Canada: *Angels, Aliens & Chariots* is a wonderful open minded exploration of scripture! Helen Glowacki brought an incredible insight to scripture which one would generally not see themselves. This book gave me the understanding that we can find answers to questions about our past and our future through scripture if we just look in the right place. This book was wonderful and I can't wait for the next one!

Susan Day, From Jupiter, Florida: *Abiding Faith, Hidden Treasure* : I hated to put it down, couldn't wait to pick it up, read all Helen's books, proves every point, shows what to do through God's words. I am 90 and Helen's books have helped me call on God.

Georgette Rothe, From Fort Piece, Florida: *Abiding Faith, Hidden Treasure* was more than I expected; a Biblical course making you re-evaluate your beliefs, enjoyed the journey very much.

Fred D'Alauro, from Palm Beach Shores, Florida: Internet 5 star rating: *When God Took Grandma Home:*Remarkable! Inspirational, moving. Fascinating storyteller with a real message.

William Dannenberger from St. Louis Missouri: *Angels. Aliens & Chariots* is a book I have not yet completed but just had to say how much I love this book so far! It presents scripture in an amazing manner and has taught me so much.

Debra Forman, Chester, New York. Internet 5 star rating: *When God Broke Grandma's Heart:* Written from the heart, shares the strong beliefs that shelters us in times of need, courage captivates the reader. Thank you.

Anonymous: Internet 5 star rating: *When God Broke Grandma's Heart:* WHEN LIFE GETS YOU DOWN, PICK THIS BOOK UP, it wrapped its arms around me. A wonderful read. Congratulations on an inspiring work.

A reviewer, a reader in Kentucky: Internet 5 star rating: *When God Broke Grandma's Heart:* Well written, heartwarming, overcoming heartbreak through God, touches your heart. A worthwhile read for all generations.

A reader: Internet 5 star rating: *When God Broke Grandma's Heart:* a must read for all generations. FANTASTIC!

A reviewer Internet 5 star rating: *When God Took Grandma Home:* Moves you, captivating.

A reviewer, a Kentucky reader: Internet 5 star rating: *When God Took Grandma Home:* MUST READ! Touching story of life's tragedies and how lessons learned from these heartbreaking events can turn into blessings.

DESCRIPTION OF CHARACTERS IN THE NOVELS
By Helen Glowacki

Grandma: Grandma's life was filled with sibling betrayal and marital abuse. Her love of God, home remedies and famous boxing stance touches the heart.

Sarah: Sarah helps Grandma write her journal, learns about God's plan of salvation and the enemy who wants to harm her. She carries on Grandma's legacy of faith.

Matt: Matt, Sarah's husband, has a rock-like faith but when he loses a loved one, struggles with his anger with God, until he has a miraculous experience of faith.

Paul: Paul is Matt's older brother who earned a Captain's license for a seagoing tugboat. His faith sustains him despite enduring terrible circumstances.

Mary and Kevin: Mary and Kevin become Matt and Sarah's neighbors and friends. Mary's panic attacks end when God brings a miracle they never thought possible.

Elizabeth: Elizabeth adopts Rebecca, loses her husband twelve years later, is confronted with a potentially deadly illness and searches for Rebecca's birth mother.

Rebecca: Rebecca is Elizabeth daughter and Jayden's friend. Her father's death, the illness her mother faces, and a series of challenges at college almost destroy her.

John: John, a deacon, lost his wife to a debilitating disease, becomes Elizabeth's friend, and helps his daughter and grandson through a difficult divorce.

Jayden: Jayden is John's grandson and becomes Rebecca's friend. He has learned that prayer helps solve problems and he and Rebecca begin to share their faith.

Wade and Ruth: Wade is Jim's boss and friend who adopts two children from Iraq. Ruth is Jayden's mother and John's daughter who struggles to let go of the past.

Joshua and Debbie: Joshua, Sarah's younger brother, was demanding and judgmental until Caleb stepped in. Debbie looks to Joshua's family to be her role models.

Caleb and Ann: Caleb is Sarah and Josh's older brother and the family looks to him as they once looked to Grandma. Ann, Caleb's wife harbors a secret sadness.

Barbara and Jim: Barbara, Matt's sister is also Sarah's close friend. Her husband Jim plays devil's advocate in family debates, and matchmaker for his friend Wade.

Heza and Bara: Heza and Bara endured a suicide bomber attack when Bara was one and one half years old and Heza as she was born. They are adopted by Wade.

Chaldeth: Chaldeth is a fallen angel sent to destroy Grandma's family. He plots to bring great heartache to Rebecca and Jayden and their family to break their faith.

Durk: Durk, abused by a cruel father, is a sophomore at the college Rebecca and Jayden attend. He brings harm to Rebecca and Jayden but Jim gives him a second chance.

Professsor T. Nagorra, and Emils, and Dean Peerca: These tenured professors befriend Durk and engage in activities that bring harm to the students and campus.

Professors Doog and Sendnik, and President Legna: These three share a faith in God, a love for their country, and desire to be role models. They help save the campus.

Richard and Rachel: Richard is a physician for whom Caleb built a house on the property next door to where he and Ann. live. Both couples share godly values and thus became friends.

Joe and Preacher: Both men work for the company which hired Caleb to supervise the construction of a shopping mall. Preacher is always trying to teach Joe what scripture says.

If a son shall ask bread

of any of you that is a father,

will he give a stone.......

how much more shall your

Heavenly Father

give the Holy Spirit

to them that ask him?"

Luke 11:11-13

ANGELS, ALIENS & CHARIOTS

HELEN GLOWACKI

www.ingramcontent.com/pod-product-compliance
Lightning Source LLC
Chambersburg PA
CBHW051520260626
47170CB00003B/708